# OFF SIDES

## Sawyer Bennett

Cover Design by Vitalink
Interior Design by Novel Ninjutsu

ISBN- 978-0-9894164-1-2

Find Sawyer on the web!
www.sawyerbennett.com
www.twitter.com/bennettbooks
www.facebook.com/bennettbooks

# ACKNOWLEDGEMENTS

I had not expected to write this book. In fact, I was all set to start on my sequel to Forever Young, but the idea for this novel just popped into my mind and would not let go. So I spent a few weeks just mulling the idea. I tried to actually write the FY sequel, but I couldn't even get started on it because this book just kept dominating my thoughts. Then I decided, what the hell. Let me just purge this from my mind.

I wrote voraciously for a solid week. 45,000+ words later, I had my first draft. I did some basic polishing and filling, but it was pretty much ready except for line edits. At this point, I'd like to give a huge shout out to Kristina Sessoms and Alyssa Shaver. Both jumped on doing a Beta read and provided great feedback, most of which I used.

Particular hug to Alyssa as she came up with the title to the book. It must have been destiny that I found her as a Beta reader as she is a huge hockey fan, a former player herself as well as a violin player. You'll see why that's important when you read this book.

As always, thank you Shawn for letting me pursue my dream. I know it means many hours that I am paying attention to my laptop instead of you. You rock my world, honey!

# REFLECTIONS

I'm not sure what possessed me to do it. Maybe it was the impossible expectations I faced, maybe it was my own self-loathing. But I just knew I needed something different to happen. I needed someone...something...to derail me from my current path.   Otherwise, I would become lost...a hollowed out shell of a man.

So I did it. I approached her, then I pursued her, then I made her mine.  And my life was saved...

# CONTENTS

# CHAPTER ONE

## Ryan

*Heh, heh, heh, heh...*

I hate those freakin' green pigs mocking me. I hit the restart button and slide my finger over the screen, pulling back the little blue bird. I let him fly, giving the screen a quick tap and my fuzzy blue missile splits into three, peppering my taunters with their rage. Ice shatters and I slaughter the green sows. Victory is mine.

"Hurry up, Ryan. Beat feet."

I glance up at the group walking ahead of me. They're all laughing, arms linked together. They look like a fucking re-run of *Friends*. We are all perfectly dressed in our designer clothes compliments of our families' obscene wealth. We have our perfect salon hairstyles and we are leading our perfect college lives. And I absolutely hate it sometimes.

Tonight we are slumming it a little. We're walking from a frat party to a 24 hour diner nearby to get some food. Oh, the shame of it all.

Between the copious amounts of alcohol and pot at the party, we all have a serious case of the munchies. Well, my munchies are just because I'm hungry. I, unfortunately, cannot partake in the cannabis laughis as the athletics department at Northeastern springs random drugs tests on its athletes. And I'm not about to jeopardize our hockey season on a little bit of reefer. I sure hope Mike and Carter stayed away from that shit tonight. I can tell by the way the girls are giggling, they were partaking.

It's 3:00 a.m. and I'm not nearly drunk enough to miss the fact that I wish I could ditch my friends and head back to my frat house for some sleep. It's been a long night and looks like it's about to get longer.

The men in our merry band constitute a portion of the first line on the Northeastern hockey team. We're all pretty tight. My right winger and best friend, Mike Yanalas, calls out to a group of young, street thugs leaning up against an old Dodge Charger smoking cigarettes. He has his arm around his girlfriend, Cameron.

"What the fuck you looking at?" Mike yells at them. He's drunk as a skunk and I sigh inwardly. I so do not want to have to back up his drunken ass in a fight tonight.

Luckily, the Crip wannabes don't say anything and slink away into the darkness. I'm not surprised, really. We are some pretty big dudes and most people would be crazy to fuck with us.

We turn onto Hay Street and we are back on my home turf. The gym where I work out is just a few blocks down and my frat house is in the opposite direction. Sally's Diner sits almost in the middle of the two points and has served as our post-party stop for the three years I have been a student at Northeastern. I break into a little trot to catch up to the others.

As we all pour into Sally's, I breathe in deeply the scent of frying bacon and french fries. The place is fairly busy even though it's the wee hours of the morn. There are several tables filled with drunken students and an old man hovering over a cup of coffee at the counter.

After pulling a few tables together, the group sits down,

pulling the sticky menus out of the placeholders in the middle of the tables. I loop my foot around a chair and kick it backwards, sliding it out from the table. I sit down and lean back, stretching my legs out in front of me. Crossing one leg over the other at the ankles, I continue to ignore the group in favor of *Angry Birds*.

I don't bother with the menu. I already know I'm going for the Husky Special. A cheeseburger with a fried egg on top plus a butt-load of french fries on the side. I've been working out like crazy getting ready for the start of our hockey season in a few weeks so I can spare the calorie overload.

"Ugh...this table is just nasty. I don't know why we always have to come here."

I keep my focus on my mission to destroy as many pigs as possible, mentally rolling my eyes at Angeline. It's irritating the fuck out of me that she's here with us and her spoiled whining is already grating hard on my nerves.

I was stunned when she showed up at the party tonight as we had been furiously trying to avoid each other since we had broken up a few weeks ago. But I suppose it was inevitable that we would see each other again, given our social circle was pretty tight. It also doesn't help that Mike is my best friend and Cameron is hers.

I sneak a quick glance at Angeline and just shake my head. She's trying to wipe the table down with hand sanitizer and napkins, a grimace plastered to her face. And watching her fret over a dirty table just reiterates to me I made the right decision in breaking things off. Angeline is just a little too prissy for my tastes. Hell, she wouldn't even give me a hug after my games until I took a shower. In hindsight, I'm surprised she didn't wipe me down with that alcohol gel of hers before we had sex. Or make me double wrap my dick with two condoms.

I pull my lower lip between my teeth in consternation. Seeing Angeline tonight was surreal. I expected her to still be furious with me for breaking up with her. Instead, she

**3**

walked right up to me and gave me a big hug, telling me that it was good to see me. I repaid the compliment, although I didn't really feel it. It was the polite thing to do.

As the night wore on, Angeline went from friendly banter to overt flirting. I didn't fail to notice the numerous times she laid her hand on my arm when she was talking to me or the way she would stand on her tip toes to whisper something in my ear.

Don't get me wrong. Tonight, Angeline is rocking a pair of skin tight jeans, a barely there halter top and some sky high heels. She is oozing sex and had she not been concentrating wasted energy on me, she would have made some other guy very happy to be having her attention.

Toward the end of the night as the band was playing one of their last songs, she tried to rope me into dancing with her. I politely declined, telling her it was probably not a good idea. She seemed to take the rejection gracefully but then promptly invited herself along when we all decided to hit Sally's. I should have just gone home but I really was starving and figured I could brave another half hour of Angeline.

So here we sit, and I'm trying to focus on slinging birds at pigs, keeping my attention half on the talk around the tables. It takes all of about five seconds for someone to mention Descartes and we are off and running.

I find it hilarious that when college students get drunk or high, we immediately start discussing philosophy. I mean, who gives a rat's ass about philosophy, but throw a little alcohol into the mix and suddenly everyone wants to pontificate.

We're all in a level 300 philosophy course called Seventeenth and Eighteenth Century Philosophers. Word around campus is that Dr. Anderson, who is about a hundred and twenty years old, basically sleeps through class and tells you exactly what will be on the final exam. The class is supposed to be a cake-walk. I sure hope so because I have damn good grades going into my senior year and I want to have an easy schedule so I can put more of my efforts into hockey.

"Well, I think dualism is a load of crap," I hear Mike say with flourish. He had a slight slur to his words. "If the mind exists independently of the brain, then how are physical memories created? Tell me how that makes sense."

"None of it makes sense," I mutter, my eyes still glued to my iPhone. No one even spares me a glance which is fine by me. My game is far more interesting that discussing Descartes.

"That's narrow sited on your part," Angeline scoffs. "Regardless, I find it more fascinating this concept of 'I think, therefore, I am'. I mean, that's pretty deep on a level I never bothered to think about before."

I am pretty sure Angeline has never thought about anything deeper than what designer jeans she will wear in the morning but I am impressed how she steers the subject away from the mind numbing philosophy of dualism.

I can see the waitress approaching from the corner of my eye but I don't look up as I am perilously close to breaking my high score. She stands there for several seconds while the conversation rages on, patiently waiting for a break in the expenditure of brain cells. When no one pauses to even take a breath, she gives a little clearing sound with her throat.

The table goes silent then I hear Angeline say in her most affronted voice, "Excuse me. But we are in the middle of an important discussion. Do you think it's appropriate to just interrupt us with the assumption we are ready for you?"

Everyone starts laughing hysterically, myself excluded. But I do give an inner smirk to myself and just shake my head. Angeline can dress someone down and make them feel about three inches tall in just a matter of seconds. It's a true art form of the criminally wealthy and insanely narcissistic.

Angeline isn't finished with her though. She turns to the rest of the table and says, "I guess we can't really fault her ignorance. I mean, she slings hash for a living. This conversation is probably a little over her head." She then breaks out into a fit of giggles that has me grinding my teeth together.

Okay, even I admit that's a pretty low blow but I don't say anything. I keep my head down, avoiding engagement with Angeline at all costs. She's drunk and she's mean. Not a good combination and I don't have it in me to fight with her tonight. Hell, that's one of the reasons I broke up with her. It just always seemed to be a fight.

Before Angeline can say anything, I hear the waitress reply, "I'm so sorry. It's just...I saw all of you sitting here, and well, forgive my ignorance, but I'm pretty sure Ockham's Razer says that among competing theories and all things being equal, the simplest theory is probably the correct one. I saw you had already looked at the menus and put them back down. Therefore, the simplest theory is that you are ready to order. Think of it this way... *I think* I saw you review the menus, *therefore I am* here to take your order. I mean, I know Ockham is a little before Descartes' time, but it's still a sound principle, don't ya think?"

There's a moment of stunned silence and my eyes snap up to the waitress. This is the most interesting thing that's happened all night...Angeline getting her spite jammed back down her throat. The rest of the table bursts out in a fit of laughter at the waitress' cheekiness and I am sure that Angeline has to be fuming. But I don't look at her because when I look at our hash-slinging philosopher, my eyes go wide and I sharply inhale. She's stunning. No, unique. No... that's not it. Uniquely stunning...that's what she is.

She has dark blond hair that she wears up in a high ponytail. She's a natural blond. I can tell by the color of her eyebrows and I'm sure if I get her pants off, I can confirm that. The bottom four inches of her hair is dyed a pale, lavender color. She is sporting a silver ring through her left nostril and a small silver barbell through her right eyebrow. She's not wearing any makeup but she has that sort of natural beauty that should remain completely unadorned. Flawless complexion with the sexiest smattering of light freckles across her nose. Her eyes are a gorgeous hazel color that I bet get greener when she's angry or excited. Right now, they are swirling with mischief and she has full, pink lips that are smirking down at Angeline.

I don't know what it is about this girl, but fuck, she's hot. And clearly smart as shit.

I've never been into girls that had facial piercings or dyed hair. The type of girls my parents expect me to date wear pearls and cashmere and have a pedigree a mile long behind their names. How does mother put it? "Your father is in the public eye so we must maintain proper appearances at all times."

My eyes rake down the waitress' body and I can get away with it because she's in a staring war with Angeline right now. She's wearing a Northeastern t-shirt and really short, shorts that showcase miles of tanned leg. She has on running shoes and sporting a little apron around her waist. Just above her right breast, which looks equally as luscious as her left, is a name tag that says, "Danny".

Miracle of all miracles, Angeline seems to have been struck dumb. Nothing is coming out of her mouth but there are daggers flying out of her eyes.

Tucking her pencil behind her ear, Danny puts her hand on her hip. "I tell you what...when you're ready to order, how about..." she pauses to look around the table and points right at Carter, "...you...just raise your hand when you're ready to order and I'll come back over and help ya out. Okay?"

Without waiting for a reply, she shoots Carter a wink and turns her back on us. I can't help it but I start laughing out loud and Angeline swings her eyes at me in fury. I ignore her, still chuckling.

"Wait, Danny," I call out. She turns around and looks at me with surprise. I'm sure she didn't think I would call her by her name. "We're ready to order. I think you've made an excellent philosophical argument."

Sauntering back to the table, Danny holds my gaze and I can see her appraising me. I don't flinch or look away, and I'm returning her gaze with equal intensity.

She walks right up to me, close enough I can smell her...and she smells like summer rain. "So, what will you have?"

She looks even better up close and I hope my tongue isn't hanging out. I want to tell her I will have her, with a side of her, and for dessert...her. Instead, I order the Husky Special.

She winks at me. "Sure thing, stud."

I hear Mike snort over that but I don't care.

She goes around the table and gets everyone's order. After her smack down of Angeline, everyone is appropriately subdued and polite. I don't think anyone wants to go head to head with this girl.

I watch her closely. Even though she was basically just called an ignoramus a few minutes ago, she seems confident and self-assured. She smiles at each of us when she takes our order, even Angeline, who is noticeably acquiescent when she orders a fruit cup and a glass of ice water. I'm impressed and find myself very curious about this girl.

Why is someone so smart working in a diner? And what possesses someone to dye their hair purple or pierce their nose? I don't get it but I find myself wanting to know.

After Danny puts our order in, conversation resumes although we're discussing hockey now instead of philosophy. I think we're starting to sober up. Mike, Carter and I discuss our season opener against Boston

College. While we are talking, I watch as Danny moves around, talking to customers. She laughs a lot and has a killer smile with a dimple in each cheek. I also notice she has a killer ass but hey, I'm a guy.

Apparently I'm not as covert as I think I am because Carter leans over and whispers to me, "She's pretty hot, huh? You thinkin' about hitting that?"

I laugh him off. "Nah, man. She's not my type."

"Well, with that body she's more than my type. I wonder if she's got any piercings we can't see."

I can't say I didn't think the same thing. Still, there really is no way I am going to find out. I can tell by looking at her she is not the type of girl that does one-night stands. Oh, she may think she's tough with her dyed hair and piercings, but looking at her you can tell she's more angel than devil. Too bad for me. And for her, too.

And a one-night stand would be the only way I could find out the answers to my questions. She definitely is not dating material because my parents would have a fit if I showed up in the media with her on my arm. This thought is disappointing to me. It's been a really long time since someone has interested me like this and now I'm all pissed off that I have to live my life by my parents' standards.

I give a silent sigh and punch Carter playfully on the arm, "Go for it, dude. Your ugly mug might have a shot with her."

# CHAPTER TWO

## Danny

I step out of my shower, shivering uncontrollably. It's the second day in a row our hot water heater has been broken and I'm getting ready to go off on the super's ass. If my roommate, Paula, and I weren't so damn poor, we'd move to a better apartment. But as it is, both of us are living hand to mouth and we just can't afford more than this squalid dump.

"Was there any hot water, Danny?"

I open the door to the bathroom and I can hear Paula in the kitchen banging pots around. I think she's making us some Ramen noodles for dinner.

"Nope. Still cold as ice," I answer her.

"Fuck. That no good fucker. Fuck."

"Language! My ears are bleeding from your potty mouth. And you owe me three cigarettes."

I hear Paula stomp down the hallway. She sticks her head in the door and hands me the cigarettes, shooting me a nasty glare. I promptly flush them down the toilet.

"You're such a bitch, Danny."

Blowing her a kiss, I reply, "I love you, too."

And I do love Paula. She is like my best friend and mother all rolled into one. We have been living together for almost two years and she's fifteen years older than me. We met working together at Sally's but she's since moved on to better things...working in a vintage record store.

Paula is a pro at cussing. I have been trying unsuccessfully since I first met her to get her to tone it down. It's not that I don't cuss, it's just that Paula does nothing but spout filthy words. So I made a bet with her that she couldn't stop using the "F" word to which she promptly sneered at me and said, "Easy Peasy". We agreed then that if she says the "F" word, she has to forfeit one of her precious cigarettes...which I happily destroy right in front of her. I figure I'll have her nicotine free before too long.

Walking out of the bathroom, she follows me into my bedroom. I drop my towel to the floor and start getting dressed.

"So, you got the late shift at Sally's?" she asks.

"Yup. I get off at 7:00 a.m."

I start getting dressed while she leans against my door jamb. "Girl, you got some crazy ass hours. Why don't you quit that fu—."

One of my eyebrows raises high to her, daring her to continuing on.

"—I mean that freakin' job?"

"Good girl," I commend her. "And get a job where? I'm a twenty-one year old junior in college with no work experience except for Sally's. Besides...the tips are pretty decent."

I thought back to the gorgeous guy who left me a fifty dollar tip a few nights ago. He was clearly a college student— probably at Northeastern—same as me. And he clearly had money if he was throwing around fifty dollar tips. I giggled thinking about that group. I knew the minute that snotty looking brunette cast her eyes on me that she was going to try her best humiliation tactics.

Luckily, she picked a subject she clearly knew nothing about and which I had done pretty well in.

Best of all was when I walked away, and the stud playing *Angry Birds* called my name. As I turned to look back at him, I almost flinched at the way he was looking at me. It was carnal...like he wanted to devour me. Just thinking about it made me blush. I glanced at him a few times while they ate, and he seemed to always be watching me. I thought about flirting a little but really, what was the use. It would never be anything more than flirting because we are from opposite sides of the track. I had tried dating someone once who was straight out of the pages of Lifestyles of the Rich and Famous and that was a disaster. Besides, I don't have the time or the energy to mess with boys at this point in my life. But maybe one day.

After the rowdy group had left, I walked over and started busing off the table. I noticed they didn't leave a tip, which was usually typical with drunk students. I suppose the only reward I would have from this table was the satisfaction of making that uppity co-ed eat her condescending words to me. I snicker again just thinking about it.

When I had picked up the last dish and started back to the kitchen, the door opened and the hotty walked back in. I watched as he walked up to me and we just stared at each other.

Slipping his hand into the pocket of my apron, he said, "Here's your tip. I forgot to leave it." The move was calculated to impede on my personal space and was incredible sexy at the same time.

"Thanks," I said softly.

He looked at me for a few seconds, then said, "Well, thanks for being a good sport tonight. You sure managed to put Angeline in her place and I'm sorry for what she said."

I cocked my head at him. "Why are you sorry? You shouldn't have to apologize for her."

He gave me a wisp of a smile and replied, "No, I guess I don't."

A few seconds passed as we just held each others eyes and I thought he might say something else. But then he just turned around to leave, calling over his shoulder, "Have a good night."

He was already out the door when I said, "You too."

It wasn't until my shift ended and I was counting my tips that I realized he left me fifty bucks. That could buy a whole lot of Ramen noodles for me and Paula.

"I'm sure I could get you on at the record store."

*Huh?* My attention is brought back to Paula and away from hot men who leave me large tips. Looking at her, I smile.

"Not if I had to dress like that," I quip.

Paula is in the beginning of her mid-life crisis. Her pitch black hair is now dyed with red streaks running through it. She cut her bangs short and severely across her forehead. The Goth look is her clothing of choice tonight and she is rockin' a short, plaid skirt in dark red and black, with a sexy off the shoulder, black top. Skull and cross-bone tights and combat boots complete her look.

"Puh-leeze, girlfriend. You are rockin' your own brand of weird with your hair and face metal. Pot...meet kettle."

I laugh as I put on my earrings and shake my head. I motion toward my face and then flip my lavender locks back. "Uh-uh. My look is pure art." Looking her up and down with my best attempt at distaste, I smirk. "You, however, are a fashion disaster."

"Bitch."

"Tramp."

"Floozy."

"Martyr."

"Strawberry Shortcake."

We both burst out into a fit of laughter. We always try to one up the other when name calling and see who can make the other laugh first. This one is a tie.

Sitting down on the edge of my bed, I put on my sneakers.

Paula walks over and sits next to me. "So, what do you have going on tomorrow?"

An inadvertent sigh escapes my lips. "Tomorrow's kind of hectic. I've got two classes in the morning and then a tutoring session at lunch. Then I promised Ann I'd fill in for her a few hours at the diner while she goes to a school meeting for her kid. And finally, I'll put in a couple of hours at the shelter."

God, my life is crazy.

Paula stands up and puts her hands on her hips. She's just looking at me, not saying a word.

"What's that look for?"

"Nothing."

"Oh, no you don't. Don't go all mommy on me."

"Well, come on, Danny. You're running yourself into the ground. I'm worried about you."

I stand from the bed and wrap my arms around Paula. "I know you're worried about me but I can take care of myself."

She squeezes me hard in return. "I know you can, honey. Doesn't stop me from worrying about you though."

I squeeze her back and then step away from her before I start blubbering like an idiot. Paula is the only one in the world I have that cares about me. Well, besides Sarge, but I just don't get to see him that often.

"I'm fine," I assure her. "Besides, this is just short term, right?"

"Sure, kiddo. Short term." She says the right words but by her tone I can see she thinks I'm in perpetual servitude.

✦

It's 3:00 p.m. and my ass is dragging. After getting off work at 7:00 a.m., I had just enough time to get a quick shower and head to my morning classes. After a torturous hour of tutoring a soccer player in Western Civ—who was more interested in trying to cop a feel than studying—I'm now at Sally's to work part of Ann's shift. Two cups of coffee and I'm feeling marginally better. Lucky for me, it's pretty dead right now.

Bending over the Classified Ads at the counter, I'm browsing for some weekend work. If I can get a few houses to clean on the weekends, that would go a long way toward helping to pay my debts.

The jingle of bells indicates a new customer has arrived. I look up, folding the paper in half and then stop. It's Mr. Fifty Dollar Tipper. And I realize I had not built him up in my mind. He is still as hot as I remembered. He's wearing a gray t-shirt that's soaked in sweat and a navy pair of running shorts. He appears to be slightly out of breath so I'm assuming he has just finished a run.

"Sit anywhere you'd like," I tell him.

He walks up to the counter, holding my gaze. There is no doubt in my mind that he has stopped in here to see me. I can tell because there is purpose and intent in those whiskey colored eyes of his.

I watch mesmerized as he runs a hand through his damp hair to push it off his forehead. It's dark brown and wavy, and bordering on just a tad too long for a mother's taste. For me, it's perfect. Too bad I don't have the time or desire to act upon it.

Taking a seat on a stool just opposite of me, he gives me a huge smile. "Shredded anyone with philosophy lately?"

I actually burst out laughing and start shaking my head. "Nope. Not today at least."

"Well, I was running by and saw you standing in here. Thought I would stop in and thank you."

My eyebrows rise. "Thank me?"

"Yup. Those twenty seconds where you were thrashing Angeline with your knowledge of philosophy was the most fun I've had in a long, long time."

It's not very lady like but I can't help snort in response. "Then you must lead a pretty dull life."

"I'm Ryan Burnham, by the way." He sticks his hand out and I shake it. His hand is much larger than mine and warm. I can feel callouses on his palms and fingers.

"Danny Cross. Nice to meet you...officially."

He releases my hand. "Likewise."

My skin is tingling where he held my hand and I immediately try to squelch those feelings. I have no business getting googly-eyed over a guy, much less one that is clearly out of my social stratosphere. I have too many other important things going on right now, or so I seem to be reminding myself a lot lately.

"So, Danny," he begins. He's looking at me with amusement, and something akin to curiosity. "You're clearly a very smart girl. Are you enrolled at Northeastern? I saw you wearing a school t-shirt the other night."

He had noticed and remembered the shirt I was wearing that night? Even I can't remember what I was wearing, and the knowledge that he held on to that detail pleases me for some reason.

"I just started this fall but I'm only taking two classes right now."

"Just two classes and you know who Ockham and Descartes are?" He's skeptical I can tell.

"I attended another school before Northeastern. I'm technically a junior."

"Where'd you go to school?"

"Nowhere important." I don't offer and decide to be elusive. I'm not sure why but I think I want to see how much interest he really has in me. It's a sick game I'm playing with myself because this is not going to go anywhere.

"Why won't you tell me the name?" He's grinning at me like a Cheshire cat.

"Why are you being so nosy?"

"Why are you being so evasive?"

I decide a rapid change in subject is warranted. "Do you want to order something? I need to get back to work."

Ryan looks around at the empty diner and then back to me. He arches an eyebrow. It's charming in an aggravating sort of way. I wait patiently for him to respond.

When he realizes the ball is in his court, he looks down at his watch and stands up from his stool. "I actually have to get going. I'm meeting a few guys at the gym."

I don't say anything—just give him a polite smile—but I am a little disappointed he's leaving so soon. He looks like he wants to say something else but he's hesitant. And as soon as I realize why he is stalling, he leans across the counter a little closer to me. "Danny...can I take you to dinner tonight? I'd really like to get to know you better."

Ah, damn. Why did this scrumptiously hot and completely charming guy have to ask me out? I was enjoying our banter, our flirting, but I never thought he'd act on it. I mean, he's Dom Perignon...and I'm Coca-Cola. And as if our differences aren't enough, I really don't have time to complicate my life with something like this.

"I can see the wheels turning in your head, Danny. I'm not asking you to marry me...just dinner."

I start shaking my head. "I don't think so. I just have a lot on my plate right now."

As I'm trying to rationalize my refusal, I'm feeling better about my decision to turn him down. I saw the friends he hung with the other night. I couldn't help but notice the expensive clothing and jewelry. The sense of entitlement that hung in the air. It's really just not my thing and why bother getting involved with someone, even just for dinner, when I will eventually never fit in. It's like taking Cinderella to the ball, but then telling her she has to go back to being a maid the next day.

Before I can start to say no again, he reaches across and takes my hand. Stroking his thumb across my wrist, he murmurs, "I didn't peg you for a chicken, Danny. Come on...just dinner tonight and we will go anywhere you want to go."

Anywhere? This could have potential. I can take the time tonight to go out with him, on my terms, on my turf, and then he will see what a bad idea this is.

The stroking of his thumb across my wrist is causing my pulse to flutter. I pull my hand away. "Anywhere I want to go, huh?"

He smiles at me brilliantly, knowing I'm about to give in. "Yes, anywhere you want."

"Okay. Meet me back here at 6:00 p.m."

He reaches back for my hand and grabs it. Before I can think to pull away, he brings my knuckles to his lips and places a soft kiss there. "See you in a few hours."

Dropping my hand, he turns and walks out the door. I watch him break into a jog and he disappears from sight. And the skin on my hand is burning slightly from the touch of his lips.

# CHAPTER THREE

## Ryan

"Why are you getting all dressed up?"

I look over at Mike who is lying on his bed with his hands behind his head.

"I've got a date tonight." I reply.

"No, shit? With who?"

I hesitate for a second before I answer and then I mentally slap myself for doing so. I am not ashamed to be going out with Danny so there should be no hesitation. Still, I'm elusive when I respond. "Her name is Danny. She's a junior here."

Mike doesn't say anything so I take it he isn't interested in hearing further. I reach into the closet and pull out a brown sport coat. I'm not sure where we are going tonight but since I told Danny I'd take her anywhere, I want to be prepared for a nice dinner if that's what she wants. I debate on a tie and then decide against it. My parents force me to wear one to so many functions that any time I can get away without one, I'm going to take it.

"So, where did you meet this girl?"

Apparently Mike is more interested than I thought. But

he has been my best friend since the beginning of high school and we've been frat roomies since we started at Northeastern. There really isn't anything I can't share with him.

"She's the waitress from the other night at Sally's."

"The hot one with the purple hair that completely knocked Angeline down about ten pegs?"

I snicker. "Yup. That's the one."

Mike lets out a long, slow whistle and is shaking his head back and forth like he pities me.

"What?" I demand.

"Come on, dude. She doesn't exactly swing in our social circle."

That just pisses me off even though I know deep down that Mike doesn't really mean anything by it.

"Why the fuck does that matter?" My words come out harsher than I intend but I don't apologize.

Holding his hands up in apology, he smoothly replies, "It doesn't matter to me, buddy. I'm just thinking about what your parents would say. I can see your mother now, *'Oh dah-ling...she has purple hair. Is she just out of prison?'*".

I bust out laughing because that is exactly what my mother would say and Mike nails his impersonation of her perfectly. This causes me to frown. Mike is correct that Danny will be shunned by my family and friends just because of how she looks. And that pisses me off all over again. And it pisses me off that I'm pissed off. I don't know this girl. I just find her interesting and want to hang with her a bit. I can't be getting angry over what my friends may or may not do in her presence when they will probably never even meet her.

"Relax. It's just dinner. It's not like I'm not bringing her home to the 'rents."

"That's what I thought. You're just trying to bang her, right?"

I angle a sharp look over at Mike and he's grinning broadly. "No, that's not what I'm trying to do. Get your mind out of the gutter, man." I grab my keys and wallet to head out. "But if she chooses to throw herself at me, I'm not going to say no."

Mike's laugh follows me out the door.

✦

Walking into Sally's I realize I'm slightly nervous. The diner is packed with the dinner crowd and I immediately see her behind the counter, ringing up someone's check.

She's still wearing what she had on earlier...jeans, a t-shirt and sneakers. Her hair is pulled up in a ponytail again and I wonder what it would look like down. I find the lavender highlights at the bottom fascinating and I'd be lying if I didn't admit I found her facial piercings kinda hot. And I suddenly realize why I'm so captivated by her. It's because she looks innocent as hell but the colored hair and face metal add a bit of rebel to that sweet exterior.

Danny glances up and sees me standing there. She holds up her index finger for me to give her a minute and I nod back. I'm happy right now just to observe her for a few minutes.

I'm struck by her easy grace. She's laughing with the customer who is paying right now and her smile literally lights up the room. The cook behind the service counter says something to her and she grimaces, throwing a towel at him that catches him square in the face. He laughs at her and all of the customers at the counter hoot and holler. She's in her element here because she is without a doubt a people-person.

Danny takes off her apron and throws it under the counter. Picking up her purse, she heads over toward me and I can feel my heart start beating faster. How in the world can someone that just finished working in a greasy diner look so damn good?

"Hey," she says. "Sorry but I ended up having to work later than I thought. I haven't had time to get showered or changed."

"Not a problem. Do you want to go back to your place so you can do that?"

She shakes her head. "We're not going anywhere fancy. Casual is better. Although, I probably smell like greasy french fries right now."

I don't know what possesses me but I step closer to her and lean my head down so my nose is right behind her ear. I take a deep breath, dramatically inhaling so she can hear me. Then I whisper in her ear, "You smell delicious to me."

And she does. Her shampoo smells like eucalyptus and orange blossoms. I actually watch as she shivers over my words and I feel like fucking Tarzan right now.

Stepping back, I turn to open the door and let her walk out ahead of me. I pull my keys out and start toward the passenger door of my black Range Rover. Glancing over my shoulder I see she's walking in the opposite direction. I put my keys back in my pocket and jog to catch up to her.

"Nice night for a walk," I remark.

She laughs and the sound warms my blood. It's rich and husky, and oh, so damn sexy.

"We're just walking to the bus stop. Tonight you'll see Boston 'Danny Style'. Although you are a little over-dressed to be riding the MBTA."

I give her a nonchalant smile. "No worries. I'm game."

She smiles back. "Good. I'd be disappointed if you weren't." Her words sound like a challenge and she has no idea how competitive I can be.

*Oh, Danny, Danny. I know what you're trying to do and you should work a little harder to be less transparent.* There is no doubt in my mind that Danny is trying to scare me off. If she thinks riding the transit bus is scary, she's clearly never had to dodge two-hundred pound defensemen to keep them from slamming you into the boards.

"So, where are we going? You said I'm over-dressed but you have to give me a better clue than that."

She just gives me an evasive smile and says, "You'll see."

I have to admit I'm now even more curious about her than before. I really kind of expected her to want me to take her to an expensive restaurant. I mean, that's usually what girls want. And the fact that she is taking us by public transit rather than using my insanely nice and ridiculously expensive car has me almost on pins and needles as to what to expect.

We don't get to talk much on the bus ride as it's packed with evening commuters. My first ride on the bus is not unpleasant though. The lack of seats means we have to stand up, and in close confines, Danny is pressed up against my side. She's holding on to a metal pole in front of her and I'm tall enough to hang onto an overhead strap with still enough bend in my arm. When the bus lurches or jostles, Danny's soft curves sway into me. A few times I place my hand on her back to help steady her and she shoots me a smirk which I return.

Finally, Danny indicates we've reached our destination and we step off with a few other travelers. It's starting to get dark and I'm a bit dismayed that we are in a fairly seedy looking area of town. The streets are lined with rubbish and I see more than one broken window on some of the buildings. I start to question Danny but she takes off across the street and I follow. We walk down the block and turn a corner, and run right into a line of people stretching out from a doorway. There has to be maybe twenty or so people in line and I'm confused. Were we at a nightclub?

Danny notices the look on my face and grabs my hand. She leads me past the line up to the front door, saying hello to a few people. And then I see a sign over the door..."Helping Hands Ministry". I glance back at the people standing in line and now I can plainly see what they are...homeless.

They range in diversity...black, white, yellow, young,

old, men and women. The only common denominator they have is that they are all poor...very, very poor apparently. Some are dressed in rags while others have dirt covering them from head to toe. I know I'm gaping at these down trodden people but I can't help myself. I finally turn my head slowly to Danny and she's looking at me like she expects me to bolt.

"I volunteer a few times a week here. It's my night tonight and I thought you could help."

My brow furrows. "And this is where you want me to take you for dinner? Not very romantic."

She doesn't say anything but just watches me carefully.

I sigh and take her hand, heading toward the door. "Well, let's get busy then."

I'm pleased when Danny rewards me with a blinding, dimpled smile as I lead her through the front door.

She takes me through a lobby area and down a flight of stairs to the basement. She points off to a door that heads into a wing of the building that she tells me houses full time residents. When I ask about the people standing outside, she tells me they are just here to eat but they live out on the streets.

Danny opens up a set of double doors and we are in a large dining hall. There are folding tables that seat eight with metal chairs around each table. I find it odd that each table has a small vase on it with a little bunch of plastic flowers in each one. Most of the seats are taken and I can see that as people finish their meal and leave, volunteers are letting more people in.

I follow Danny around the perimeter of the room to the back where there is a service counter which reveals a large kitchen behind it. A swinging door to the side allows people to go in and out between the kitchen and dining area.

"It's about damn time you got here, Danny. I'm up over my ass in trying to get the food prepared for tomorrow."

"Chill out, Maverick. I'm here now and I brought help. But we both expect a good meal after we're done."

Danny looks at me and I mouth the word, *Maverick*?

She leans in and whispers, "Top Gun is his favorite movie."

I look over at Maverick. He's Asian and extremely short. He's wearing an apron over his clothes that's spattered with food and he's stirring a large pot on the stove. The hat on his head says, "Honey Badger Don't Care".

Danny opens a drawer and pulls out two aprons, throwing one at me. "Mav, this is Ryan. He's my wingman tonight."

I hate to admit, I don't appreciate the Top Gun reference. The wingman is supposed to help the other person get laid and I'll be damned if I'm going to help Danny do that.

Maverick looks at me, taking in my clothes. "He's dressed kind of fancy. Are you sure he can get his hands dirty."

Before Danny can answer, I say, "I'm sure I can get my hands dirty. Tell me what to do."

Mav just grunts at me but points to a pile of potatoes on the counter. I take my coat off and hang it over a chair, rolling my shirt sleeves up. After placing the apron on, I pick up a potato and start peeling. Danny comes up to stand beside me and starts helping. We work in companionable silence, mainly because Maverick is standing there and I'm thinking he might fillet me if we are not diligent in our duties.

When he leaves the kitchen, carrying the large pot that was on the stove with him, Danny leans her body toward me and gives me a nudge with her shoulder. "So, how are you doing?"

"Awesome. I love peeling potatoes. It's one of my favorite things in the world to do."

"First time, huh?"

I laugh. "Yup. But I always like to try new things so I can mark this off my bucket list."

We're both quiet for a minute, and then I say, "You know, Danny...bringing me here won't prove anything."

She looks at me and I can see shock on her face that I figured out her motive. She starts stammering about not trying to prove anything, but I wipe my hand off on a towel and place my finger over her lips. I lean in a little and murmur softly to her, "Don't deny it. It doesn't become you."

Her eyes are wide and confused, all for about three seconds then she bursts out laughing. "I guess I'm not going to be able to pull any fast ones on you."

"I got your number," I reassure her.

We talk about mundane things while we work as there is just no opportunity for deeper conversation. I do find out that Danny has been volunteering here a few times a week since she was sixteen, which also leads her to confirm that she's a Boston native like me. Maverick bustles back and forth between the kitchen and dining area, bringing in dirty pots and serving pans. While the residents and street guests actually clean their own dishes and utensils at a washing station in the dining hall, the lovely duty of scrubbing the cookware falls to me and Danny.

After two hours of peeling potatoes, scrubbing pots and hauling garbage, I realize my back is actually a little sore. That surprises me because I'm a pretty fit guy. You can't play NCAA hockey and not be in top shape. I don't know how Danny does this twice a week and I'm finding myself respecting a girl for something I've never really experienced before in the opposite sex.

Dedication.

This is a crappy job and she actually volunteers to do it. It kind of humbles me.

I'm wiping down the last counter top and I look over at Danny. She's holding my sports jacket out to me. "You did great tonight. How about letting me buy you a beer?"

I put the cloth in the sink and take my apron off. Taking my coat from her, I drape it over my arm. I hold the other one out to her and she hooks her arm through it.

I smile down at her as she looks so freakin' adorable right now, her arm linked with mine. "I asked you out so the beer is on me."

# CHAPTER FOUR

## Danny

I'm impressed. Ryan has taken this like a champ. I fully expected him to pitch a fit when I told him we were riding the bus. I was ready for a tantrum when he saw the area of town we were in. And then I waited for him to bail when he realized we were working at a homeless shelter on our date. But he did none of those things.

Instead, the bastard kept a smile on his face and seemed to eagerly enjoy the work we were doing. And I say bastard because I also fully expected to finish this date tonight and we would go our separate ways. Now, I have to admit to myself I'm intrigued by him and more than a little attracted to him. I mean, I was attracted to him when I first saw him, but only in the way you see a really hot guy and think to yourself, "that's a really hot guy" and then you go on your way.

But now, I really want to know more about him. I'm attracted to him in a way I don't want to be.

I should have never asked him for a beer but here we are, back near campus and sitting in a popular hangout called *Neely's*. The waitress takes our order. I ask for a Bud

Light and Ryan orders a Sam Adams and a plate of nachos.

"Nachos? Didn't that delicious bowl of soup satisfy your hunger tonight?" I tease him.

"I will agree that was one delicious bowl of soup we ate tonight, but it in no way was enough to fill me up."

I watch him frown after he says those words and his brow furrows deep.

"What's wrong?" I ask.

He shakes his head for a second, staring at the table. Then he looks up at me and my heart actually flips a little at the tortured look in his eyes. Now I'm concerned. "Ryan, what's wrong?"

"It's just...I make a flippant remark that the bowl of soup wasn't enough to fill me up. Then I order a plate of nachos. Those people back at the shelter...that bowl of soup is all they are getting tonight. I just realized..."

Our waitress arrives with the beers and sets them down. I'm glad for the slight interruption so I can collect my thoughts. Poverty and homelessness is not an easy subject to discuss.

"And you're feeling guilty." I don't ask it as a question but state the obvious. "Which is okay, Ryan. I feel that way too a lot of the time."

"I admire you a lot, Danny. Your commitment is...inspiring."

I take a sip of my beer and give a smile of thanks. "Well, the cause is a bit personal to me. My dad was homeless and he died out on the streets."

I'm not sure why I told Ryan that bit of personal information. I guess I didn't want him thinking that everyone had to be as involved as me. I didn't want him carrying guilt. And now he's looking at me...and his coppered eyes are swimming with...pity? No, that's not it. Sympathy. Definitely sympathy.

"What happened?" he asks softly.

I shrug my shoulders as if it's not a big deal, but it is. My dad fell down a spiral of despair and hopelessness that not even the love of his family could pull him out of. I took another sip of my beer and leaned forward with my arms resting on the table.

"My dad was a cop here in Boston. He worked narcotics and unfortunately, had a dirty partner. He got my dad dragged into stealing drugs from evidence and re-selling them on the streets. It was only a matter of time before they got busted and when they did, my dad's life was over for him."

It's funny how I can talk about him now without experiencing blinding pain because there was a long period where I couldn't. But as with all things, time can dull the hurt.

Ryan reaches across the table and takes my hand. He gently runs his thumb over the top while he holds it. "How did he end up homeless then?"

"His life just unraveled. First, he was fired. Although the DA cut him a deal to avoid prison time if he turned state's evidence against his partner and the other people involved, he was humiliated beyond repair. He started drinking... heavily. He became depressed. Ultimately, he started using drugs... hardcore stuff like heroin. Eventually my mom had to ask him to leave the house. He did but being unemployed and an addict, he ended up on the streets."

Ryan squeezed my hand. "I am so sorry, Danny."

I give him a squeeze back. My eyes are dry because I have no tears left for my dad. I try now to remember only the good about him. "It's okay. It took me a long time to come to peace with it."

The waitress arrives with Ryan's nachos. She sets them on the table and gives us each a plate. I watch as Ryan takes a heaping pile and I pick one up to nibble at it.

"How did he die?" Ryan asks.

"Well, he actually got into Helping Hands Ministry and tried to clean himself up. In fact, the last memories of my dad are me going there to visit him. He actually was sober for a few months but then relapsed. He went back out on the streets, peddling drugs and eventually he got shot in a deal gone bad."

Ryan is silent for a minute. And it's okay. It's not uncomfortable and I watch him pick at his nachos. Finally, he pushes the plate aside and leans forward, crossing his arms on the table. He looks directly in my eyes with a seriousness that makes me swallow hard.

"I'm beyond sorry—."

I cut him off by holding my hand up. I give him a genuine smile. "You don't have to be sorry. I'm serious when I say I made my peace with it."

Ryan is shaking his head back and forth, and the look on his face is sad. "No, listen to me. I'm sorry because before tonight...I never once thought about any of this. I'm not sure I've even seen a homeless person outside of TV. And I am feeling all kinds of bad that I didn't bother to notice. But I'm grateful that you showed me something new tonight. Something everyone should see."

Ryan pauses and looks down at the table. My heart breaks a little for him because I can see that his ignorance of these issues is causing him some real pain. I don't know what to say to him. I feel clueless and all of a sudden, I'm thinking how very bad this evening is turning. Because I'm starting to feel something for this man sitting across from me and it's the last thing in the world I want right now.

And yet, I'm helpless when I reach across the table and take his hand in mine. With my other hand, I stroke the back of his, running my fingers lightly over the crisp hairs. I turn his palm up and trace my index finger over his callouses, reveling in how they feel against my soft skin. With my thumb, I trace around the outer edge of his thumbnail, almost absentmindedly while I think of something comforting to say to him.

I sneak a glance up at him and my breath catches. He is looking at me with such startling intensity that I drop his hand.

"Don't," he rasps. Then he clears his throat. "Don't stop touching me."

I am mesmerized by his look and I think I might go up in flames right now. The hunger in his eyes...for my touch, my approval...is overwhelming. I tentatively pick his hand back up and start touching him as he asked. I feel a connection to him that words can't describe at this point. I'm sure I'll spend a lot of time later analyzing it.

I opt for a change of subject to ease the tension.

"So, why do you have all these callouses on your hand?" I realize how that sounds and start snickering. "I mean—that is—if you can tell me in polite company."

Ryan pulls his hands back and snorts at me. He pulls his nachos back over and tucks in. "They're from playing hockey."

"Do you play inter-mural or something?"

His smile at me is one of indulgence. "I play for Northeastern. I'm the captain of our team."

I choke on the swallow of beer that was heading down my throat but is now headed for my lungs. Ryan patiently waits while I hack and cough to clear my throat. He actually smiles at me while he's chewing his food, patiently waiting for me to catch my breath.

"You're the captain of the team? The Northeastern, NCAA, Division I hockey team?"

I can see he's enjoying my shock.

"Sure am. Are you a hockey fan?"

"Uh, hello...born and raised in Boston. Of course, I'm a hockey fan."

Ryan gives me a smirk but rather than want to slap his face, I want to run my fingers along his jaw. He has dark stubble gracing the hard lines and it makes him look dangerously sexy.

"Well, for someone who is such a hockey fan, how come you didn't know I am the captain of your school's hockey team?"

"Touché, Mr. Burnham...touché." I give him a mock

salute.

He pops another nacho in his mouth and gives me a wicked grin. "That's Captain Burnham to you." I just roll my eyes at him and take another sip of my beer. This time, it goes down smoothly.

✦

Ryan is driving me to my apartment now and I'm brooding over what has occurred. I agreed to go out with him tonight thinking he would be scared away from someone like me. Not that I think I'm deficient in any way. It's just we come from two vastly different worlds. We are definitely not "peas and carrots".

However, I have found Ryan Burnham to be more than the pretty face that first caught my eye. He's funny, charming, kind and in no way the stuck up prig I originally thought he might be.

I so don't want to like him but I do. And now I don't know what to do with it.

Ryan pulls over and parks on the street outside of my building. I start to open the door but he lays his hand on my arm, stopping me. I turn to look at him and I've immediately lost the war that was brewing in my head mere seconds ago. He lifts a hand up and smooths it over and past the hair at my temple until he is cupping the back of my head. He doesn't make a move but just holds me by the head, looking at me. I nervously wet my lips which immediately draws his attention there. He brings his other hand up and gently traces my bottom lip with his thumb.

"Do you think this is a good idea?" I whisper. I want him to say yes. I want him to say no.

Ryan drags his gaze up from my lips and looks at me. "I don't know. I can be all kinds of fucked in the head sometimes."

Is he warning me off? Should I listen?

"Who isn't fucked in the head these days?" I ask.

"Indeed," he murmurs as he bends his head toward mine.

Our lips meet softly...nothing more than a whisper against each other. Moving to my cheek with his other hand, Ryan holds both sides of my head and presses into me. His tongue slides gently into my mouth and at the first contact, a groan bubbles up from my chest. My hands involuntarily fist in his shirt and I attempt to get even closer to him. I am being swallowed by his kiss and it's all I can do to hang on.

Ryan pulls slightly away and I make a whimper of dismay. But he only moves his mouth to the corner of mine, placing soft kisses from there along my jaw. With a slight tug of his hand on my ponytail, my head tilts to the side and he blazes a trail kisses along my neck. His lips are soft and warm and when he hits my collarbone, I'm completely enslaved. If he told me to take off all my clothes right there, I probably would have. Instead, he pulls away from me and lays his forehead against mine. His breathing is as heavy as mine and I now understand how car windows become fogged.

"Come on. Let me walk you to your door."

Ryan opens my car door for me and takes my hand. We walk together to my apartment door and I'm looking for my keys in my purse, all of a sudden nervous. A minute ago I was ready to jump in bed with Ryan, but now, in the harsh fluorescent light of the hallway outside of my apartment, I'm faced with the uncertainty of a relationship with a man who is so different than me.

Putting his finger under my chin, Ryan tilts my head up to his and says, "Don't."

He knows I'm doubting this and that tells me a lot about how perceptive he is. Before I can respond he pulls me to him and kisses me...hard. And every thought flies out of my head.

My hands snake up his chest and wrap around his neck before slipping into his hair. It's as soft and silky as I had been trying hard not to imagine. Our tongues are swirling...stabbing...and then my teeth grab his bottom lip and bite. He answers me with a guttural sound that vibrates from his mouth into mine.

Without breaking our hold on each other, Ryan pushes me one step backward until my back is pressed into my door. His hands graze down my sides until they reach my hips. His fingers dig in, pulling me tight against him and I can feel his hardness. I am drowning in Ryan, or maybe he's downing in me by the sounds of his ragged breathing, I do not know. I just know I have never been kissed like this before and something warm is unfurling in my chest in response to this passion.

Ryan finally pulls away slightly, breathing hard against my mouth. "Jesus, Danny."

I don't think Jesus has anything to do with the explosion that just happened between us but if He did, I'm heading to church this weekend to thank Him.

"I better go," Ryan says against my mouth, his lips still pressed lightly to mine.

I nod my head shakily and I can't even form a word. I think he blew a gasket in me or something.

Pulling back, Ryan reaches into his pocket and pulls out his phone. "What's your number?"

I give it to him and he types it into his phone. My phone immediately starts ringing and I look down. He's called me and I grin.

"So, now you have my number too," he says.

# CHAPTER FIVE

## Ryan

The alarm blares at 6:30 a.m. and I slap it off. I wake up with a smile on my face as I had an amazing dream about Danny, the dirty details I will not disclose.

I think back to our kiss last night. Never before had a kiss turned me on like that. I was close to begging Danny to let me bury myself in her. But at the same time, I didn't want to go further. I wanted to savor it all. And this morning...I realize I want to drag it out. The way she stroked my hand last night, in comfort of me, after all she has been through...words can't describe. I want to take my time with this girl because she is so different than anyone I have ever been around.

Rolling out of bed, I see Mike is still asleep. I pick up a pillow and throw it at him.

"Get up, Petunia. We have to be at practice in half an hour."

Mike groans and slowly sits up. His blond hair is sticking up all over the place. "How can you be so chipper this early in the morning?"

"Just excited to get on the ice."

"Why do you have a dopey grin on your face?"

He's trying to get a rise out of me but I don't respond. "I'll see you there. I'm going to grab something to eat first."

"Hold up, man."

I pause and look at him.

"So, how was your date last night?"

"It was fine...nice. Do you want me to wait for you?"

"Yeah, I'm getting up." Mike swings his long legs out of bed, stands and stretches. I pull out my iPhone while Mike gets dressed and think about sending Danny a text. Should I make it short and flirty? Or should I send a more romantic text. Oh my God...I'm turning into a putz, but then I smile and roll with it. Just as I'm ready to type, Mike gives me a punch in the shoulder.

"I'm ready."

I put the phone in my pocket and pick up my gear bag. I'll text her after practice.

✦

I'm sitting in the locker room, getting ready for practice. I've got my Under Armour, jock shorts and shin pads on. As I'm pulling on my hockey socks and securing them to the Velcro tabs on my shorts, Mike walks over and sits down on the bench beside me.

"Alright...I can't stand it. Spill."

I don't look at him. "Spill what?"

"Don't be an ass. Just tell me how the date went. Usually you're willing to tell me everything but you are keeping this one close to the vest. I figure that means it went really, really well or really, really bad." He stands up and moves in front of me. He pounds his fist into his chest. "I'm here for ya, man. Whichever way it went."

I chuckle at him. "Okay...fine. If you must know, it went really, really well."

Mike sits down again, crossing one leg over the other in

feminine fashion. He puts his hands on his knees, gazing intently at me. "Do tell."

I snicker and throw a roll of tape at him. I stand up and pull my pants on. "I don't really know what to say. She's amazing."

"Whose amazing?" This from Carter who walks up behind me.

"No one," I say at the same time Mike says, "His date from last night."

I groan. I so don't need Carter in on this conversation. I love the guy but he has a big mouth.

"What date? Where have I been?"

Mike pipes up. "He went out with that smokin' hot waitress from Sally's."

I sit down to put my skates on, pulling the laces tight.

"Dude," Carter says. "You said you didn't want to hit that." His voice sounds accusatory and I remember back to that night. Carter acted like he might try to ask her out.

"I'm not 'hitting that', Carter. We went out on a date."

"But you said she was amazing. If you didn't bang her, what was so amazing?"

I grab the tape off the floor and start wrapping my shin pads. "Carter, you are such a Neanderthal. Not everything is about screwing."

"Yes, it is," Carter replies matter-of-factly. "I mean, what could have been more amazing last night than screwing?"

Carter is genuinely curious I can tell and it's sort of endearing. He may be a player right now but I bet one day, Carter is going to fall hard.

"You guys are like pit bulls. If you must know, I went with her to a homeless shelter and we did some volunteer work in the kitchen. Then we went and grabbed a couple of beers."

Carter is looking at me as if I just sprouted antlers out of my head. "No, seriously...what did you really do?"

I just shake my head and pick up my shoulder pads,

strapping them into place. "Forget it, Carter. I just don't think you'd understand."

He is literally scratching his head in consternation as he walks away. I turn to look at Mike. "Was my date last night really that weird?"

Mike stands up and slaps me on the shoulder. "Yup. It was weird. But it was also amazing, and that's all that matters. I'm happy for you, man."

I punch him lightly in the chest. "Thanks, bro."

✦

Practice is almost over and we are doing a light scrimmage right now. I'm the center on the first line and I've been playing fucking fantastic today. I'm on a breakaway right now, having just received the puck from a brilliant pass by Mike. I'm streaking down the right side, and Mike is mirroring me on the left. There's only one defenseman between us and the goalie. I make a quick pass over to Mike. Just as the defensemen commits to Mike, he flips the puck back to me and I wind up for a slap shot, aiming for the five-hole. Just as I'm bringing my stick down toward the ice, I see the blade of another stick poke between my legs and hook over the front of my left skate. It's jerked backward, along with my foot and I go crashing face first into the ice. I'm moving so fast the momentum slides me head first into the boards. Thankfully, I'm able to tuck my head and catch the boards with my shoulder instead.

The coach blows the whistle and I hear Mike bellow, "What the fuck, Malone?"

I didn't need to hear Mike yell to know it was Reece Malone who had pulled me down. He is a loser and I don't understand why Coach keeps him on the team. He's bitter that his talent will never get him higher than our fourth line and he begrudges success to anyone else. Even if that means our team takes a loss. He is poison to our morale.

I jump up from the ice and take off toward Malone. I'm going to kick his ass. I hear the coach frantically blowing the whistle and my teammates rush in to separate us before we can even connect.

"You try that shit again, Reece and I will tear your fucking head off, you hear me?"

I am pissed and if I didn't have three of my teammates holding me back, I probably would have killed him. Reece just smirks at me. He shakes off the hands holding him and skates off the ice.

Coach wisely calls an end to practice and we all head to the locker room. As I walk in, I move past Malone who is standing in front of his locker and try to ignore him.

"Hey, Burnham. I heard you went slumming last night and banged some grease whore from Sally's."

I vaguely hear Mike say, "Oh fuck" but then all I hear after is the sound of my fist hitting Malone's face. I get in at least four good hits, all to the left side of his temple and jaw, before Carter and Mike are pulling me off. No one needed to hold Malone back because my hits were vicious and fueled by an inferno of rage. He is on the floor, blood running down his face from an open cut, and he won't be getting up anytime soon.

Mike is pulling me backward and tells me to calm down. I shake him off of me viciously. "Get the fuck off me, Mike. I'm fine."

He pulls his arms back and holds them up in surrender. He looks at me apprehensively.

I turn my back on him and stalk over to my locker. Coach comes up to me and gives me a dressing down. He tells me to get my ass in gear or else I can kiss my Captaincy goodbye. My only consolation is that Malone needs five stitches in his head.

✦

By the time Mike and I make it to the dining hall, I've calmed somewhat but my stomach is in knots. I was beyond furious when Malone called Danny a whore. I try to imagine what she would have felt like if she had heard that. And now I'm afraid that Danny will be facing an endless stream of spitefulness from my crowd just because of her lot in life.

I grab a tray of food, not really paying attention to what I'm choosing. Mike and I find an empty table and sit down.

"You okay, man?" Mike's eyes are filled with concern.

"Sure."

"What's up with Malone? It's like his attitude is getting worse. I don't understand why Coach doesn't kick him off the team."

I shake my head. I don't get it either. But if Malone is going to tear our team apart, we can kiss any chance of a winning season goodbye. I eat in silence, mulling everything over.

"Hey, Ryan. You know what Malone said about Danny is just words, right? They shouldn't mean anything to you."

He's trying to comfort and reassure me, and I get that. But a dark feeling is taking root in my mind. I'm not sure I'm ready for this. I don't know if I can handle the inevitable fallout that is going to come by forging a relationship with Danny.

"This is a bad idea...to get involved with her, isn't it?"

Mike shrugs his shoulders. "Maybe not."

"You said it yourself. My parents will never accept her because she looks different and isn't in our social haven. Our crowd has their heads so far up their asses, they believe because she works in a diner that she's a whore. Tell me how this can work?"

I feel like I'm almost pleading with him to give me the right answer.

Mike puts down his sandwich and leans forward. "Tell me, Ryan...do you care what she looks like?"

**41**

"No, although I think she's freakin' gorgeous."

"So, her purple hair and nose ring and...whatever that is in her eyebrow...that doesn't bother you?"

"Not at all."

"And the fact she works in a diner? Does that change how you feel?"

"No! I admire the fact she's working...two jobs...going to school and doing volunteer work. She's amazing."

"Then I don't see what the problem is, dude. All that matters is what you think."

I sigh. I know that. And I don't care what anyone else thinks about me for being with Danny. But I do care if Danny gets hurt because of the nastiness I'm surrounded by.

Danny and I have been out one time. We've spent less than three hours together, and yet I find myself wanting to protect her more than any other person I've ever known. The strength of these feelings scares the shit out of me. I just don't know what to do.

# CHAPTER SIX

# Danny

It's 6:00 a.m. and my alarm is shrieking from across the room. I put it over there so I have to get up and get out of bed to turn it off. Otherwise, I'm always in danger of just falling back asleep. I put my pillow over my head and try to ignore it. When that doesn't work, I throw my pillow at it and it makes a direct hit, knocking the clock to the floor. Except, it's still shrieking at me. I simply take my other pillow and cover my head with it.

It's been five days since my date with Ryan and he hasn't called me. I'm depressed and I know it, and I hate myself that I feel this way. I should have more fortitude than I'm showing right now.

I spent the day after our date replaying everything over in my mind. I spent a lot of time thinking of our last kiss. I couldn't help but imagine what comes after a kiss like that. In theory, I know what happens after a kiss like that. In reality, well...let's just say I have to rely on my imagination.

When I had not heard from Ryan the day after our date, I was a little worried and slightly annoyed. I sent him a quick text the following morning:

**Hi. R U ok?**

He texted back fairly quickly.

**Yup. Something came up. Call u later.**

I immediately felt better after getting his text and went about spending another day waiting for him to call. Except, rather than walking on clouds and day-dreaming about our phenomenal kiss, I obsessed about why he had not called. I had a nagging feeling that something wasn't quite right. Thinking of every possible reason why he wouldn't call, I was convinced by the end of that second day I would not hear from him.

And I didn't.

No calls, no texts. Nothing.

I didn't bother to text him again. A stalker I was not.

By the end of the third day with no word from him, I deleted his contact information from my phone.

The alarm is still shrieking and Paula's bedroom door opens. "What the fu-u—udge, Danny? Turn that damn thing off."

I ignore her and the alarm. Lying here in bed and ignoring everything is what's on the agenda today. I have a blessedly rare day to myself with no work obligations, no school and I plan on having a date with my pillow.

My door opens and footsteps pad across the floor. The alarm turns off and there is now oppressive silence. My mattress dips down and I know Paula is lying in my bed beside me. I don't move.

"Are you just going to lay here?"

"Yes," I mumble. "And I'd appreciate it if you leave me alone."

Paula is silent for several seconds and then the pillow is ripped off my head and the covers are pulled back.

"Alright. I've had it with you. You are no longer allowed to sulk, pine, mope, pout or glower. You're going to get your ass up and get back on with your life."

I roll over and look at Paula. She is grinning at me, completely unapologetic for her vigorous tactics to get me

**44**

out of bed. I couldn't help but to smile back at her.

"So how are you feeling, kiddo?"

Flipping in the opposite direction, I roll completely off the bed and stand up. Stretching my arms upward, I give a huge yawn. "I'm fine. Besides, you know I'm really not one to lie around and bemoan anything. It is indeed time for me to move on."

"True dat. I've never met anyone that tries as hard as you do to get past something hurtful."

I grimace at her words. They are true but they make me sound callous. Whenever anything bad has happened to me, I tend to grieve pretty hard but then I tuck it away and try not to look back. That has worked well so far dealing with both of my parents' deaths. Not so well with the loss of my music. And the jury is still out how I am going to let Ryan's brush-off affect me.

Gosh, I so want to just kick my ass right now for falling so easily for that man. I knew better! I have a very specific agenda to complete certain things in my life, and I have no business getting sidetracked. That includes going gooey over a hot hockey player who kisses like Armageddon is just on the other side of the horizon.

"I think I'm going to go for a run this morning. Want to join me?"

Paula snorts at me. No matter how many times I've invited her to run with me or workout, she always has the same answer. "Let's see...running or cigarettes? I choose cigarettes."

Giving her a good eye roll for measure, I head to our tiny bathroom to brush my teeth. It's definitely time to move on.

◆

Heading out of my apartment, I see the sun has already risen but it's still quite chilly. The decision to wear my light weight running jacket and long pants is smart. I plan on doing five miles today so I will probably be burning up by the time I get back.

Opening the front door to my building, I'm setting the timer on my watch as I jog down the front steps. Not paying attention to my surroundings, I'm brought up short in surprise when I hear, "Hello, Danny."

My head snaps up and I lock onto Ryan's eyes. Even as I feel anger rush through me, I also have a tremor of excitement over seeing him. I quickly take him in. He's standing there with his hands tucked into his incredibly well fitting jeans' pockets. His hair is perfectly mussed and hanging boyishly over his forehead.

"What are you doing here?" I ask.

Even as pissed as I am at him, I'm surprised that the words come out as just merely curious and I'm glad. I don't want him to know he affected me the way he did.

Ryan frowns at me and it's clear on his face that he did, in fact, suspect he'd get anger from me. "I was hoping we could talk."

I look up and down my block, considering if I should just bolt forward into my run. But curiosity is getting me. "How long have you been here?"

"Since about 5:30 a.m."

My eyebrows shoot up. "Hard time sleeping?"

"Something like that," he murmurs. "I wanted to talk to you and I didn't want to miss you coming or going as I didn't know if you were working today, so I just decided to camp out."

That's interesting and should be slightly flattering he would do that to make sure he could see me. But I quickly tamp that feeling down. *I will not fall back under his spell*, I repeat to myself over and over again.

"Look, Ryan...you don't owe me any explanation or anything and frankly, I'm good. There's nothing to really talk about."

Anger flashes through those bourbon colored eyes.

Score one for a direct hit.

"Didn't the other night mean anything to you?" he demands.

I cock my head slightly at him because it's certainly weird that he would be affronted by my lack of interest since he's the one that didn't call me as promised. "Didn't it mean anything to you?" I retort.

He runs his hand through his hair in a measure of frustration. Sighing, he whispers, "It meant more to me than even I suspected. That's why I need to talk to you."

Something about the earnestness in his words melts a little bit of the ice. He's not giving me a line and I sense it is important for him to tell me something so he can ease his burden. Why I am taking it upon myself to let him do so remains to be seen.

I sigh. "Fine. Do you want some coffee?"

"Sure. That would be great."

I turn and walk back into my building with Ryan on my heels. He doesn't say anything but that doesn't stop me from being painfully aware of his presence behind me. There's like a disturbance in the atmosphere when I'm near him.

When I open the door and we walk into the apartment, I take off my jacket and throw it over the back of the couch. He follows me into the kitchen.

I pull out two cups and fill them up. I push his cup toward him and indicate cream and sugar which he declines. Just as he's taking a sip, I hear, "What the fuck is he doing here?"

I look behind me and Paula is standing there glaring daggers at Ryan. Not saying a word, my hand reaches out to her palm up. She turns her glare to me then grabs her purse off the counter, fishing around inside. Coming out, she quietly lays one cigarette in my palm. I stick it under the kitchen sink and soak it with water.

As I throw it into the garbage, I hear Paula say, "Pardon me. May I inquire as to what this gentleman is doing in our apartment?"

I glance over at Ryan and he's looking at Paula like she was the bearded lady in the circus...a mixture of grotesque curiosity and humor.

"He's here to talk for a few minutes. I'm choosing to indulge him." I pick up my coffee cup and walk into the living room. Taking a seat on the couch, I watch as Ryan folds his large frame into an old, tattered wicker chair. Our furniture is second hand and mismatched as all get out. Paula walks right in behind him and sits down next to me on the couch. She's still glaring at him and now he's glaring back at her.

"Paula...it's fine. Give me a few minutes alone to talk to Ryan."

She reluctantly stands up and moves around the coffee table to leave. Pointing her finger at him she says, "I'm watching you, boy."

I can't help but snicker. Paula is five foot nothing and weights ninety pounds soaking wet. But boy can she be scary when she wants to. Ryan does nothing more than give a small nod of his head in her direction then turns his eyes to me.

I settle back into the cushions and take a sip of my coffee, watching him over the rim. He scrubs his hand through his hair which I now see is definitely a nervous gesture. It unsettles me that I immediately take note of how his hair slides forward, lying in gentle waves along the side of his temple and neck. I remember how soft it felt as I ran my own fingers through it not but a few days ago. I sigh at myself. I really need to let the hotness of Ryan go.

Leaning forward, Ryan puts his elbows on his knees and clasps his hands together. He looks at me and there is sorrow there. Here comes the apology and I try to steel myself against it.

But I'm caught off guard when he doesn't apologize. Instead, he says, "The morning after our date, I woke up thinking about you. And I was almost giddy with happiness." He gives me a small smile. "Then I went to hockey practice and one of my teammates called you a whore."

I flinch backward from the softness of his voice and the hurtfulness of his words. Why would someone view me that way?

Before I could say anything, Ryan continues,"I beat the shit out of him until he was bleeding all over the locker room floor."

Oh wow. I feel slightly vindicated. "Did you get in trouble?"

Ryan shakes his head while looking down at the floor. Then he drags his eyes back up to me. "At first, I was furious someone would say that about you. My best friend, Mike...he said it shouldn't matter. It only matters what I think about you."

"Sounds like Mike is pretty smart," I muse.

Ryan leans back in the chair, laying the palms of his hands on his thighs. He starts picking at, what I assume is imaginary lint, just to keep his hands busy. "Yeah, he is. But, the fact of the matter remains, that if we date, there are going to be people in my circle that will think that. Some might even say that...right to your face. And...I just didn't want you to have to go through that."

"So you decide on your own that a relationship is not a good idea...to what...protect me?" I'm pissed I didn't get a say-so in this and I'm sure he can tell by the tone of my voice.

Ryan sighs and pinches the bridge of his nose. He looks like he had a major headache brewing. "Here is where I need to be absolutely honest with you, Danny. Yes, at first my thoughts were solely about protecting you. I didn't want you to get hurt. But then I started realizing that I would get hurt too. Every time you would get hurt, I would hurt as well. And I then questioned whether I was able to make that type of commitment to someone. I'm ashamed to say...I was protecting myself, too. I didn't think

I was ready for this."

His words hurt but I also have to admire and respect his brutal honesty. He could have sugar coated this breakup to me but he candidly tells me that he's afraid for himself as well. "I get it and I appreciate the truth. I know you could have given me a dozen lines to help ease your conscience over this."

"I'm glad you understand," Ryan says as he stands up from his chair.

So this is it, the final goodbye.

Except...he doesn't head toward the door. He walks right over to me and sits beside me on the couch. As I turn to face him, he reaches out and strokes his fingertips over my cheek. I shiver as the rough feel of them gently caresses me.

"I'm glad you understand that because I expect you to understand this as well. It only took me another two days to realize that I would rather suffer the pain of what others might think than be away from you. It took me two more days to get up the nerve to come here to see you. The only thing I can ask of you is can you endure that with me so we can try again."

I close my eyes as his thumb gently plays along my jaw. I let his words settle into me and I enjoy the warmth they promote...for just a minute. But then I push past it. It's probably a really bad idea to even entertain the notion of a relationship with Ryan.

So far, he has proven to be skittish and apparently runs in a circle of assholes. Do I want to even be involved in this?

I open my eyes and look at him. Before I can even say anything, he leans in and brushes his lips over mine. He moves his mouth to my temple and presses a light kiss there. Then he whispers, "Please. Take a chance."

I pull slightly away from him. I'm wary but I cannot deny that I feel an intense connection to Ryan. It is more than just physical attraction. I sense something in him that resonates with me although I cannot put my finger on it. Am I willing to explore that further to see if it can be identified?

"Okay," I breathe out.

"Okay?" Ryan sounds bewildered.

I nod my head and before I know it, he wraps me in a suffocating hug. Ryan presses his head into my neck and murmurs a "thank you" against my skin which causes my pulse to go through the roof.

Pulling back he looks at me. Cupping both of my cheeks with his hands, he just stares at me with such ferocity that it makes me want to devour him. I lean in to kiss him but he stops me. "I'm so sorry I hurt you, Danny. I won't do it again."

I give him a smile before I lean in to claim that kiss. "Okay. I'll hold you to that."

# CHAPTER SEVEN

## Ryan

I must be the luckiest son of a bitch on the planet right now. Danny is willing to give us another chance and I feel like I just won the Stanley Cup.

We are sitting on her couch having just finished an awesome breakfast that Paula cooked while Danny took a quick shower. She never did go on her run and I'm glad. I didn't want to miss a minute with her today.

Turns out, Paula's not so bad. She can be scary—terrifying actually—but it's in a protective way for Danny and I'm all for that. Turns out, she had been standing in the hallway the entire time we talked, so she overheard everything. She made a big entrance as we were kissing to let me know that she forgave me too.

How comforting.

At least I can be fairly sure she didn't poison my pancakes.

Paula has left to go to work and we now have the apartment to ourselves. Danny has a rare day off from all of her obligations and we decide to just stay here today and chill out. We have a few days of lost time to make up for and I want to know everything about her.

Danny is sitting on one end of the couch with her back against the armrest and her legs curled underneath her. She's wearing a pair of old, faded jeans that hug her curves just right and sports a hole in one knee. Her t-shirt also hugs her amazing upper body curves and I can't help periodically glancing at the words "Kiss Me – I'm Irish" stenciled across the front of her breasts. She's barefoot and her toes are painted a deep purple color which I find to be incredible sexy.

I'm at the other end of the couch and my legs are extended with my feet resting on either side of her hips. "Okay, first things first...what is Danny short for?"

She laughs at me and it's music to my ears. If I could make a full time job out of listening to Danny laugh, I would.

"Daniella. But no one calls me that. Ever," she says with warning.

"Why not? It's a beautiful name."

She shrugs her shoulders at me. "I don't know. It's always been Danny so that's what I'm used to."

"Fair enough. So what's with the purple hair and piercings?"

She grabs a lock of her long hair, pulling it over her shoulder and looks down at it in reflection. "You don't like it?"

"On the contrary, I love it. I mean, I've never gone out with a girl with colored hair or a nose ring, but I have to admit...it's hot as hell on you. It's what makes you unique. And I'm finding a new fondness for unique things."

She giggles at me. "It's a good thing. Because I wouldn't change it for you."

"And I wouldn't ask you to."

She flashes me a smile that is so genuinely happy, that my breath catches. Her teeth are straight and gleaming white. Her dimples are perfectly etched and her lips could have an entire book of poetry written to them.

Holy shit! I was becoming a fucking dork thinking like that. Still, I had to admit that her beauty had me a little captivated. Okay, a lot captivated.

"How did you get into hockey?" she asks, breaking into my thoughts before they can veer into all the things I would love to have her do with those poetic lips.

"Gosh...let's see. I've been playing since I was about six years old. My uncle played in the NHL back in the 80's and he's the one that originally got me into it. I played Junior Hockey before being recruited to Northeastern."

"Do you want to play professionally?"

I lean forward and grab both of her ankles, straightening her legs out. Her feet rest just short of my crotch, which is a good thing. I pick one dainty foot up and start massaging it, working my thumb into the arch. She gives a little groan and closes her eyes, and holy hell that is sexy. I shake my head to clear my thoughts.

"Yeah, that's my dream. It will go against everything my parents expect of me, but that's what I want."

"Do you always do what your parents expect?"

"Not always but I have a lot of the time."

I don't elaborate but she's not going to let it go. And honestly, I don't want her to let it go. I want her to want to know about me. She pushes on. "And why do you do what they expect a lot of the time rather than what you want to do?"

"My dad is Alex Burnham."

I'm watching her face as I say that and I see the recognition immediately dawn. "You mean Congressman Alex Burnham?"

I nod my head at her. "The one and only. He's so far to the right I keep expecting for him to disappear over the horizon." I know there is bitterness in my voice and she picks up on it immediately. My dad is hot in the Republican party right now and he has his eye on the White House. It's the main reason my parents want to control every aspect of my life. They want the perfect looking family that will survive a media blitz during election time.

"That's a lot of pressure on you, huh?"

"You have no idea. It's always been about what is best for our family's public image. It's about me dressing the right way, having the right education, marrying the right debutante." I pause my ministrations and lay the one foot down, picking up the other. "My dad expects me to go to law school after I graduate."

She's silent for a minute and then she asks, "Do you have any chance of getting into the NHL?"

I realize she has to ask me this because she has no clue if I'm any good or not. I don't like tooting my horn, but I want her honest opinion. "Yeah, I am. I missed entry into the draft last year because I was out most of the season with an injury to my shoulder, but that's fully healed now. I'll be an unrestricted free agent when I graduate. There are a few teams that have shown interest."

She's impressed, I can tell. I feel the need to clarify. "I might not see any ice time and may even have to play in the minor leagues, but right now I am playing some of the best hockey of my life so the recruiters are calling."

"Well, then to me it's a no brainer. If you have even the smallest chance of pursuing your dream of a hockey career, you have to take it now. Law school will always be there but hockey won't necessarily."

She makes it sound oh so simple but she's never had to deal with the fallout that occurs when I go against even a simple wish of my parents. Still, it's a pretty rebellious move dating someone like Danny so maybe I need to continue this trend.

"I'll take that under advisement, Miss Cross."

She smiles at me and we both lapse into a short period of comfortable silence. After massaging her foot for another minute, I place it down. She looks at me with tenderness in her eyes and I flip positions to crawl my way across the couch to her. The look in her eyes turns dark as she watches me approach.

"Mind if we take a break from talking?" I ask.

She gives her head a small shake in the negative which makes me grin at her. She wants my touch as much as I want to give it.

As I move over top of her, she leans back and scoots a little down so she's lying on the couch. I stretch out over the top of her, holding my weight off of her with my arms. We just look at each other and the minute she glances down at my lips, it's all over.

I crush my lips to hers and she lets out a startled moan but she opens her mouth to draw me in. Jesus...she tastes like heaven and I can't stop the groan that is rumbling up from me. A jolt of pure lust shoots through my body and I instantly harden. And she knows it as my hips are lying in between hers. I keep my lower half perfectly still as I don't want to turn into a fifteen year old boy that dry humps his pillows.

I slow the kiss down and explore her mouth more leisurely. This is good because while my lust is in no way cooled down, I am getting back a measure of control. Danny's hands grip my biceps and she flexes her fingertips inward as we kiss. I can't wait for the day when those fingertips will dig into my ass as I'm making love to her, but that day is not going to be today. I do want to take this slow for her. I have no idea what her level of experience is, and frankly, I don't care. I want for both of us to come together when the timing is perfect, and with our relationship so new, today is not that day.

I pull my mouth away and she whimpers, putting her hands around my head and trying to drag me back down.

"Danny, you're not making this easy," I grumble.

She gives me that husky laugh. "Who says I want to."

Oh, God...I'm a goner if I don't put some distance between us. I have never gotten so worked up over a girl so quickly. I press a quick kiss to her lips and stand up from the couch. She has disappointment written all over her face.

"Danny...I want nothing more than to have sex with you right now..."

"But..." she prompts.

"...but, I want this to be special. I want you to know that I'm willing to wait until it's right. I want it to be perfect for you."

She stands up from the couch and has such a hauntingly beautiful smile on her face. Her dimples slightly wink at me. She steps into my body, wrapping her arms around my waist and laying her cheek against my chest. My arms go around her and I squeeze. After placing a kiss to the top of her head, I rest my chin there.

Glancing around her living room, I see several pictures on the end table. One is of a man in a police uniform who I assume to be her dad. I pull out of her embrace and walk up to the assembly of photos.

Danny comes to stand beside me. Bending over, she picks up the one I was looking at. "This is my dad, Clayton Cross. This was taken a few years before he got fired."

I look at the picture. I can see she inherited his dimples as he flashes a toothy grin at the camera.

She puts that picture down and picks up another. This is of a gorgeous woman in her forties and there is no doubt she's Danny's mother. They look like sisters.

I take the picture from her to look at it more closely. The resemblance is uncanny. "There's no mistaken where you get your looks from."

She gives a light laugh. She takes the picture back, gently rubbing her fingertip over it. "That's what everyone says. Her name was Rosalyn."

I jolt in stunned disbelief. "Was?"

I just assumed Danny's mother was alive. Why, I don't know. Maybe because she had told me her dad was dead, but never mentioned her mother. I just assumed wrong.

"She died almost two years ago. Glioblastoma multiforme. It's a very aggressive and usually fatal type of brain cancer."

I don't know what to say. Her words are filled with sadness but she is not painfully grieving. If anything, she is speaking with such a fondness for her mother that I ache for her to speak of me that way.

She puts her mom's picture down and picks up another that I had not noticed. It's of Danny. She's wearing a long black gown that is fitted to her body. It has short sleeves and a very demure neckline that gives no hint of the cleavage below. Danny's hair is a bit shorter, just at her shoulders, and it is streaked with red and black color. She has the nose ring and eyebrow piercing and in all other ways looks the same. It couldn't have been taken that long ago.

I take all of that in but it is not what is most interesting about the picture. What catches my eye and holds it is the fact that Danny is holding a violin in one hand and its bow in the other.

She plays the violin and I'm astounded.

I look over at her and she's enjoying the look of shock on my face. "That was taken my first year at Julliard."

My mouth falls open in astonishment and I look back at the picture. "You were just as beautiful then, but I think I'm partial to the purple hair," I murmur.

Her laugh washes over me and she takes the picture back and sets it on the table. Taking my hand, she pulls me into the kitchen. "Let me make lunch for us and you can ask me any questions you want. I can see them floating all over your face."

I sit down at the counter and watch as she pulls out stuff from the fridge to make sandwiches. Her back is turned to me and I just stare at her for a second. She so beautiful, and complex, and damaged...and yet she's about the most joyful and giving person I know. It is incomprehensible to me and I realize I have something to learn from this girl. Being in Danny's presence makes me realize my life has been pretty lackluster.

"So, tell me more about your mother."

She puts all of the sandwich stuff on the counter and a smile lights up her face. "Oh...let me tell you...Rosalyn Cross was a handful. She was one of the funniest people I've known. And she was beautiful, and kind, and smart."

I watch as Danny puts our sandwiches together while talking. She never misses a beat which tells me that it is both natural and comfortable for her to talk about her mom.

"When my dad spiraled down, she stood by him as long as she could. She loved him passionately. But she wasn't going to let him impact negatively on my life so she made him leave." She pauses and looks me in the eye. "It was the bravest thing I'd ever seen in my life."

I cannot even imagine the sacrifice that Danny's mother had to make to ensure her daughter was safe. I can't imagine what it was like for Danny to love a father that was totally self-destructive. And yet, here she is with deep and abiding love for both of them.

Sliding my sandwich across to me, she turns to pull a beer out of the fridge and holds it up. I nod and she twists the cap off and she hands it to me. "I can't get over how much you two look alike."

"Yup. She always called me her 'mini-me'." She has a dreamy look on her face as she is soaking in that happy memory.

Danny takes a bite of her sandwich, chews and swallows "The thing I will always be the most grateful for was the way she encouraged me to be me. My mother was athletic and I know really wanted me to play sports. But I loved music and because I loved it, she encouraged me to be passionate about it. When I wanted to pierce my eyebrow when I was sixteen, she let me do it. Because she knew I craved individuality. I would not be what I am today if it wasn't for her."

"Then I owe your mom a debt of gratitude because there isn't any part of you that I'm not insanely attracted to."

Danny gives me a shy smile and continues eating.

"So, tell me about Julliard. And particularly why you are not there anymore."

Danny nods her head up and down while she is chewing. After she swallows, she picks my beer up and takes a sip. "So, I applied to and got accepted there. I want to get my Bachelor's in Music. And, well...I loved it there, of course. Music is what I'm meant to do. But when mom got sick, I had to drop out and care for her. It took her only eleven months to die after her diagnosis but it was long enough that I lost my scholarship. And after, dealing with mom's funeral and all of her medical expenses...it just wasn't feasible for me to return."

"When you say feasible...you mean it wasn't affordable?"

"Yeah. It's just not affordable right now. I sold my mom's house and got a little money from that, but I'm working to get the rest of her medical debt paid. I'm taking a few classes now but I'll try to get back into a music school once I get back on my feet. It might not be Julliard but I'll find somewhere that will work."

She gives me a brash smile, and again...I'm amazed at her positive spirit and outlook. How in the world did this incredible creature survive it all? Losing both of her parents, in horrific ways, and then losing her music education. And still, she smiles and keeps on truckin'? I mean, who does that? Before I can even think if it's wise to do so, I find myself offering.

"I can help you, Danny. Pay for the expenses."

Her eyes snap to mine and I see a brief moment of fear in them. And then it slips away and she gives me a genuine smile. "No, you can't. This is something I have to do. But you have totally melted my heart that you offered."

I try to give her a smile but it fails. I don't want her to have to do this on her own. I want to help...to protect her...to bring her joy. And why am I feeling this way? I barely know this girl and yet...I feel closer to her than I ever felt to Angeline in the two years we dated.

I get up from my stool and walk over to her. Her eyes are wide as I put one hand behind her head to cup it. Her eyes are more green today than hazel and I hold them. "I didn't make that offer lightly, Danny. I have an incredible trust fund at my disposal and if you need the help, I'll give it. Even if you want to call it a loan. With that said, I understand if you need to do it on your own, too."

Danny reaches up with her hand and runs her finger tips over my bottom lip. It is a surprisingly sweet gesture but still has the power to practically bring me to my knees.

"Thank you for understanding", she says.

And then she replaces her fingertips with her mouth.

# CHAPTER EIGHT

## Danny

I'm falling and I'm falling hard. I'm at work right now and I'm just counting down the minutes until I see Ryan. He's going to come by here when I get off and then we are going over to my apartment to hang. Which loosely means to make out.

That makes me smile. And feel flushed. The attraction I'm feeling for Ryan is unbelievably insane. He only has to look at me in a certain way and I'm ready to shed all my clothes.

We hung out in my apartment all day yesterday until he had to leave for an evening hockey practice. We spent some of the time talking, and we watched a movie. And the rest of the time we spent fooling around. It was awesome and it is frightening the speed with which I am becoming lost to this man.

I frown remembering our conversation when he offered to help me with mom's medical expenses. I had a brief moment of panic.

For just a moment, a fear so intense coursed through me that my stomach knotted up. His offer to help me was made without reservation, without expectation of something in return, and was made solely because he wanted to help me. It was the sweetest, kindest, most selfless thing anyone has done for me in a long time and that in and of itself scared the shit out of me.

There...I said it...I'm afraid of what Ryan Burnham can make me feel. I'm afraid because I barely survived the trauma of losing my mother and my music education all in one fell swoop. I've since that time purposely avoided things that could hurt me again. And let's face it...falling in love is a risky venture.

But I cannot ignore the fact that I feel very alive when I'm around Ryan. The barest trace of his fingertip across my skin makes me squirm. The timber of his voice can make my pulse flutter. He has come into my life for a reason and I've decided that I just can't turn my head if that bitch Karma wants to pay me a visit. I think I'm due for a measure of happiness. I just hope Ryan is that measure.

"Hey, gorgeous."

I spin around and my mouth instantly waters. Ryan is standing there wearing a pair of dark jeans that hang low on his hips. He has on a charcoal gray, long sleeved Henley. His hair is artfully unkempt and I want to run my hands through it.

"Hi, back at ya."

"You about ready?"

I nod and take off my apron. I step from behind the counter and all of a sudden, I'm shy. I look down at the floor but then he's tilting my chin up with his forefinger. When I meet his eyes, he swoops down and gives me a sweet kiss. One of the customers at the counter hoots his approval and I pull back with a huge grin on my face.

As we drive the short distance to my apartment in Ryan's Range Rover, he holds my hand the entire time. Before he pulls over to park, he brings my hand to his mouth and gives it a kiss.

"My fraternity is throwing a party tomorrow and I was wondering if you would come with me? If you don't want to, we can do something else. But I'd really like you to come and meet some of my friends."

I squeeze his hand and grin at him. "Are you sure? This will be our first step out into public."

He shoots me a smirk. "Of course, I'm sure. I really want you to meet Mike and some of the other guys on the team. The non-asshole ones. But, I can't promise everyone will be nice. So are you ready for it?"

"Sure, why not. And besides...I have it on good authority if anyone speaks bad about me that my boyfriend will beat the shit out of them."

Ryan laughs as he pulls over into a parking space. Putting the car in park, he leans across the console and gives me a scorching kiss. He pulls away and I'm breathless.

"What was that for?"

"Because that was the first time you called me your boyfriend and it turned me on."

"Oh," I say as I rub my bottom lip that's still tingling from his assault. "Then let me just say...boyfriend, boyfriend, boyfriend!"

Ryan bursts out laughing and pulls my face to him. He resumes his kiss and I am aching and needy when he draws away again.

"Come on," he says opening the car door. "Let's go get something to eat."

◆

I whip up an easy dinner of spaghetti and garlic bread. This is quite the splurge from Ramen noodles. Ryan insists on washing the dishes and I happily sit on the barstool watching him while he works.

For such a large guy, he moves with fluid grace. I can't wait to see him on the ice. I also can't wait to see what he looks like without his clothes. God, I am turning into a hussy. But even as I think that about myself I am admiring the way his shirt molds to his frame. There is not much left to imagine as to the cut of his chest, arms and stomach.

We've only known each other a few days but there is not a doubt in my mind that I am going to give my virginity to Ryan. I just don't know when it will be. Like Ryan, I am savoring the anticipation and I figure we will both know when we just can't stop the momentum. When that time comes...I'll be so ready. I'm all grown up now and I am with someone that completely rocks my world.

Ryan dries the last plate and puts it in the cupboard. Turning toward me, he leans back against the counter, his hands gripping the edge beside his hips.

"Can I ask you a favor, Danny?"

"You just cleaned my kitchen and I hate that chore more than anything so I'm in your debt. Shoot."

"Will you play your violin for me?"

Oh, why did he have to ask that?

Tears immediately well up in my eyes and I see panic fire across Ryan's face. I turn and sprint for the bathroom before he sees me break down into a sobbing mess.

I no sooner close the door and make a dash for the tissue when Ryan is knocking on the door.

"Danny...what's wrong? Please, what did I say? I'm so sorry...I didn't mean to hurt you."

Oh, his sweet and kind voice is hurting because I am hurting and the floodgates open. I start sobbing and sink to the floor with my back against the door. I know Ryan can hear me crying but I can't stop.

"Danny...please let me in."

I have for so long hidden my grief from others, that my first inclination is to bar him from seeing me this way. But all of a sudden, I have the most overwhelming urge to sink myself into his embrace so I can have just a bit of help to ease the pain.

I immediately jump up and open the door, falling into his arms. He wraps himself around me and puts his lips to my hair. He is whispering words of comfort, soothing away my pain. "It's okay" and "I'm sorry" and "What can I do to make this better?"

And all I can do is cry and cry and cry.

Ryan eventually picks me up and carries me into the living room. He sits on the couch with me in his lap and continues to soothe me. I lay my head on his chest and let him and I revel in the cocoon of understanding he is giving me.

My tears eventually dry but Ryan continues stroking my hair, my arms, my face. He kisses my temple, my cheek and the corner of my mouth, then squeezes me in a hug. I have never felt so cherished in my life.

"I'm sorry," I eventually mumble.

"What for?" he asks gently.

"For being a basket case."

He chuckles. "Well, I have heard a rumor that women are prone to fits of emotion at times."

I laugh into his chest and take in a deep breath. God he smells good. His cologne is subtle but spicy and it exudes masculinity.

I pull back and look at him. "I can't play for you because I don't have my violin anymore. I had to sell it to pay for some of the medical debt."

Ryan gives me a look of horror, understanding and sympathy, all rolled into one, and my tears threaten to build again. He pulls me back to his chest and hugs me. "I'm sorry, Danny. Can I do anything for you?"

I know what he is asking me. If he can get me a violin, but he won't come out and say it. I shake my head.

But then I pull back and put my hand to his cheek. "Actually, you can do something."

"What? I'll do anything."

I give him a wicked smile. "I want you to take me into my bedroom and make me forget about my music for tonight."

Ryan's inhales sharply and I swear his copper eyes turn amber. As I sit in his lap, I immediately feel the growing evidence of the affect my words have on him and it makes me feel incredibly powerful. He searches my eyes as to some clue of what I really want but I don't offer a hint.

Ryan takes my face in his hands and pulls it close to his. "I'm not making love to you tonight, Danny. But if you let me, I promise I will take your mind off your music for a while."

I give a little sigh and nod my head.

"Please," I whisper.

Ryan shoots off the couch with me in his arms and walks down the hallway. I point to my door and he pushes it open with his foot. I have a bedside lamp on with a red scarf thrown over the top and it provides incredible romantic lighting. That certainly wasn't my intent when I had originally put that scarf there months and months ago, but hey, that works out wonderfully.

Ryan puts one knee on the bed and lays me upon the top. I scoot over to make room for him and he follows me.

We both lie down and face each other, and for just awhile, we lay there and look at each other.

Finally he brings his hand to my face and then curls his fingers around the back of my neck. "You are so beautiful, Danny."

"I could say the same about you."

He gives me a hint of a smile but then his look turns molten. He leans in and kisses me gently. I follow his pace, soaking in the experience. I know I'm not losing my virginity tonight but I know I'm going to learn something new and I am tingling with anticipation.

Before long, our kisses turn more urgent. I feel like I am spinning out of control and Ryan masters my mouth. He commands it and it obeys him. My tongue and his move together and then apart. Needing to be together, then needing to roam.

Ryan's hand grabs a hold of my waist and he pulls me closer to him, his fingers digging deliciously into my tender skin. He brings my pelvis flush with his and he groans when we make contact.

Sliding his hand up the back of my shirt, he gently caresses my back while moving his lips to my neck. He's driving me crazy and every point of contact is burning where he touches and then freezing when it leaves. I'm in sensory overload and when his hand moves around to my front and gently cups my breast, I'm almost embarrassed over the guttural moan that escapes my lips.

"Ssshhhhh," he soothes me, yet his hand fondles me with more urgency and I want him to slip it beneath the barrier of my bra.

All of a sudden, Ryan pulls back and I am bereft. I reach toward him and he takes one of my hands and kisses my fingers.

"I'm not going to make love to you, Danny." I'm not sure if he says this to convince himself or me. "But, I would like to see and touch more of you. Will you let me?"

*Oh, yes, please*, I want to scream but I just nod my head dumbly. I don't think I can even speak a single word at this point as my vocabulary seems to consists of groans and sighs.

Before laying back down with me, Ryan sits up on his knees and reaches his arms up to pull his shirt over his head. My tongue about falls out of my mouth. His body is even more beautiful than I had imagined. His chest is smooth and defined. His abs are washboard ripped and there is a dark trail of hair that starts just below his navel and dips down into the front of his pants. I reach my hand out and run my fingers through it. Ryan hisses and I start to pull my hand away, thinking I've done something wrong.

He grabs my hand and holds it there to his stomach. "Don't stop. That felt good. Really, really good."

Oh, damn. The fact I can make this gorgeous man hiss in pleasure nearly has me swooning.

I eagerly spring up to my knees and move in closer to him. I reach my hands out and realize my fingers are shaking. I look up at Ryan and he is gazing at me with unfettered desire in his eyes. I place my right hand over his heart and his skin is hot. I can feel the mad thumping beneath increasing in speed and power. Running my hand down his stomach, I lean in and place a soft kiss on his chest and Ryan groans. When my hand reaches the waistband of his jeans, I start to go lower but Ryan pulls my hand away and puts it behind my back, holding it there.

With his other hand he grips my head and nearly incinerates me with his mouth. Something decadent starts to spread through my body and I want more.

Releasing my hands, Ryan swiftly pulls my shirt over my head and then pushes me back on the bed. My breath is coming in ragged puffs and I hope I don't hyperventilate. The look on Ryan's face is almost feral and it excites me beyond all measure.

His gaze rakes over my breasts which are heaving in their B cups and down my stomach. He stills when he reaches my belly button and sees the piercing that is there. It's a simple barbell but one end has an aquamarine crystal ball glittering in the lamplight.

He runs his fingers lightly over it and then looks at me. "Any other piercings?"

I shake my head with a shy smile.

"Good. I don't know if my heart can take any more sexiness."

I grin, thrilled that he finds pleasure in looking at me.

Maneuvering until he's kneeling in between my legs, his hands reach the button of my jeans. He looks up at me. "Can I?"

"I'll die if you don't."

Ryan pops the button and slowly slides the zipper down. He's no longer looking in my eyes but looking to see what is revealed below. I lift my hips up so he can slide my jeans all the way off and I feel wanton and free at the same time.

When I am wearing nothing more than a simple white bra and bikini bottoms, Ryan kneels at the end of the bed and just looks at me. I know I should feel self-conscious but I don't. The look on his face is utterly transparent and I know at this moment that I am the most beautiful thing he's ever beheld.

Ryan covers me with his body and our mouths fuse once again. I feel like I am drowning but I don't want it to stop. I'd happily drown if this is what it feels like. My breathing gets more shallow as Ryan moves his way down my body. Dragging his lips and tongue in between my breasts, he pops the center clasp and peels the material back. Alternating between his tongue and his fingers, he pays me exquisite care. Quickly, I am moaning up a storm but I can't stop myself. I have a feeling that when we finally do the act, I'm going to be a screamer.

While his lips continue to drink at my breasts, Ryan moves his hand down to the front of my underwear, skimming his fingers over the top. My hips buck at the slight touch and Ryan practically growls over my responsiveness. Making his way back up my throat with his mouth, I cannot be distracted enough when Ryan slips his hand inside my underwear and proceeds to touch me in the most carnal of ways.

I am beside myself. If Ryan's lips were not licking, sucking or biting mine, I would be thrashing my head side to side. I can feel pressure building inside of me and it scares and excites me all at once. The pleasure is almost painful, yet I must see what comes next. Tears form in the corners of my eyes and then suddenly I'm splintering into a million sparks of light while Ryan's mouth quiets my cries of surrender.

When I return to earth, Ryan is still gently kissing me. He gathers me in his arms and pulls me close. I am boneless and my heart rate is starting to decrease. I suddenly feel a lethargy overtake me and I cannot keep my eyes open. Before I know it, I'm asleep with my head lying on Ryan's chest.

# CHAPTER NINE

## Ryan

I'm driving to Danny's apartment to pick her up for the frat party. I'm excited and nervous. I cannot wait to see her.

Last night was amazing. It was one of best sexual experiences of my life and I didn't even get off. Watching Danny though—watching her break apart under my hands—was an incredible rush and I know beyond a doubt that when we actually have sex, it will probably shatter me.

I'm nervous about how my friends will treat her. I know Mike and Carter will be respectful and I even know Mike's girlfriend, Cameron, will be nice—as long as Angeline isn't there to taint her.

I actually like Cameron. Mike met her our freshman year at Northeastern and they've been together ever since. He's confided in me that he's going to pop the big question on graduation night. He's asked me to help him look at engagement rings in a few months.

Cameron is the one that introduced me to Angeline. She thought we would be perfect together and we were—on paper. Oh, there was a time when I was hot and bothered by Angeline. What nineteen year old guy isn't around a gorgeous college girl. And in the early months of our relationship, we actually got along very well. Once my parents checked out her pedigree, they fell in love with her and my mom was constantly talking about what beautiful babies we'd make.

But over time, the shine wore off. I have a theory that when you start dating someone, you are always on your best behavior. As you get more comfortable with a person, you start relaxing your guard and letting your true self shine through. The one thing that rang through too loud and clear for me with Angeline was her shallowness.

Oh, in our circle she was fine. Angeline comes from the richest of rich in New York City and she is used to the finer things in life. And when people get in her way who are not worthy, she has no problem in letting them know it. I guess if I had to admire anything about her, is at least she's honest to people's face when she says something about them. She doesn't hide behind whispered gossip.

Our relationship met its demise when one evening, as we were kissing on my bed, I literally couldn't get excited for her. It may have been because just two minutes before she was whining because her daddy didn't buy her a diamond necklace that she wanted, or maybe it was the way she made fun of our assistant coach's disabled son. But something in me just snapped and the attraction I held for her was gone.

Angeline did not take the break up well. She cried and begged. Then she screeched and threw things at me. Then she cried some more before finally threatening me. It was brutal but once she walked out of my room that night, I felt utter relief and I knew I had made the right decision.

Here's the thing about Danny. She's seen me at my worst already. I hurt her for no good reason other than protecting my own heart and she forgave me. And I know how vulnerable she is but it doesn't scare me. I want to protect her. In all the months I had been with Angeline, I never had the desire to put her needs above my own, yet that is all I can think about with Danny.

✦

We arrive at my frat house and we know the party is in full swing because we can hear the beat of the music inside of my car. I open Danny's door and she steps out. She is simply stunning even though she's wearing just a simple pair of jeans, a dark green blouse and black boots. Her hair is long with large waves running through it. She's wearing no makeup except her lips look shiny with gloss and I want to kiss them. I pull her to me and instead kiss the tip of her nose.

"You put every woman on the face of this earth to shame, Miss Cross."

Danny giggles. "I want to jump your bones too, Mr. Burnham."

I bust out laughing and pull her in for a hug, rocking us back and forth while our chuckles wind down.

Kissing her fingertips, I lace mine through hers and we walk in. I take her up first to my room so I can show that to her. I took a few minutes to clean it up, which basically meant I had to throw all of Mike's dirty clothes into the closet. The guy is a complete slob.

Danny walks around the small room, looking at all of the hockey photos and memorabilia I have. She asks if I have a pictures of my family and much to my chagrin, I don't. My parents aren't the casual-photo type of people.

Before we walk out, Danny sits on the edge of my bed and bounces up and down a few times. I look at her quizzically and she gives me a saucy wink. "Just seeing how loud it squeaks."

"You're rotten, you know that?" I ask.

"I know it."

Back downstairs, I get us each a beer and we make our way over to Mike. He and Cameron are talking to Carter.

As we approach, I put my arm around Danny's waist to make it clear to anyone and everyone that she is with me. I told Mike I was bringing her tonight, and he in turn told Cameron to be on her best behavior. But Carter is definitely surprised.

I make formal introductions and we all make small talk. I had told Mike that Danny was a music major which gives him something to talk about with her as his mother is an executive in the music business with Sony. I sit back and just enjoy watching Danny's naturally effervescent personality win Mike and Carter over. When Carter steps away to get another beer, he punches me in the shoulder and snarls in my ear, "You're a bastard for getting her before me."

I grin at him. He doesn't need to tell me how lucky I am.

Cameron is being polite and actually engages Danny in some small talk about Julliard. Then to my surprise, she asks Danny about her piercings because she was thinking of getting her belly button done. That leads to a fifteen minute discussion about piercings that actually leaves me a bit nauseous about the whole thing. I'll admit I'm a wuss.

The evening was going better than I had expected. All of my friends and teammates are being very nice to Danny, which isn't too hard once they get to know her. Again, she could win anyone over.

At one point, I get called away by Carter who wants me to help him get one of our drunk fraternity brothers up to bed. He apparently vomited his guts up and was passed out in the downstairs bathroom. Danny assures me she is fine hanging on her own.

When I return, my stomach churns because I see Reece Malone talking to her. And he is all up in Danny's personal space. I can tell by her posture that she doesn't like how close he is and unfortunately, I can tell he is drunk. I know I will have to handle him with kid gloves so he doesn't make a scene.

Coach had an "intervention" with me and Reece the other day, and basically demanded that we kiss and make-up. Under Coach's glaring eye, we had to shake and grumble apologies to each other. It did nothing to cool the animosity between us but at least we were putting on good appearances.

I walk up to where they stand and I notice from my peripheral vision that Mike is walking over to join us. I decide to play casual so as not to incite Reece. Walking up beside him, I clap him on the back and say, "Hey, man. How's it going?" I even manage to plaster a smile on my face that I hope doesn't come across as fake as it feels.

Reece looks at me skeptically but then sticks his hand out to shake. I grasp it and give it a quick pump, then immediately step over to Danny. While I am all for being nice to Malone to avoid a confrontation, I still want to make it clear that Danny is mine. Looking down at her I see relief in her eyes and my blood instantly boils because I know he must have said something to make her uncomfortable. I place a quick kiss on her temple then turn back to Malone. His eyes narrow at me.

"So, you ready for the opening game next week?" God it's painful trying to make conversation with this guy.

He doesn't respond but turns his gaze back to Danny. I can see understanding dawn on his face. "Hey, you're the girl that works at the diner, right?"

I feel Danny stiffen beside me and before I can launch myself at him before he says something hurtful, Mike is there pulling Reece away. I hear Mike say, "Hey, Malone. I need you to come over here and settle a bet between Carter and me over who the leading goal scorer was in the NHL last year."

I take a deep breath in and let it out. My blood pressure starts coming down and I turn to look at Danny, ready to apologize.

"That guy is a fucking, asshole," she says before I can say a word. Then her face instantly colors red and she has a sheepish grin on her face. "Oops. Sorry. I normally don't use that word."

"Did he say something to upset you?"

She shakes her head. "He was just drunk. No worries."

I start shaking my head back and forth with a smile on my face. Danny isn't stupid. She knows Malone is the guy that had called her a whore and yet she's standing strong. I'm not sure if this girl ever lets anything get her down.

I lean down to kiss her. "You're incredible...you know that?"

She gives a little moan of appreciation against my lips. "Mmmmm...you're my... boyfriend, boyfriend, boyfriend."

"Yup. Still a turn on." And I kiss her more deeply.

She laughs against my mouth and I have an overwhelming and sudden urge to yell out to the world that Danny Cross is my girl. All I need now is a caveman club and I will be complete.

It's getting close to midnight and we need to leave. Danny has to be to work at Sally's early. We purposefully didn't drink that much tonight since she has to work and I am driving. We make our goodbyes and I am pleased when Mike and Carter both lean down to give Danny brotherly hugs. They have welcomed her into the fold. While Cameron doesn't give her a hug, she does shake her hand and tells her how nice it is to meet her. That's at least a start.

Just as we are approaching the door to leave, we're brought up short by Angeline who steps right in front of me and plasters herself to my body. She throws her arms around my neck and is hanging on like a leech. I have to release Danny's hand so I can peel Angeline's tentacles off of me.

Holding her wrists, I push her back away from me and I instantly see that she's drunk. When I release her hands she starts swaying back and forth.

"Come on, Ryan. That's no way to treat an old friend." Her words are slurred and I'm afraid she's going to fall over. Which might be good. At least we can step over her and make our way out.

I sigh. "If you'll excuse us, we are just leaving."

Despite how drunk she is, she moves surprisingly fast and steps in our way as we try to walk by her. Turning her beer goggled eyes to Danny, she focuses on her. "Hey, I know you. You're that waitress from Sally's."

Danny sticks her hand out to Angeline. "That's right. I'm Danny Cross. It's nice to formally meet you."

I'm amazed. Danny is actually trying to be polite to her. She has more self-control than I do. Angeline just looks down at Danny's hand and curls her lip up in a snarl. "As if I'd shake hands with someone like you. And before you think you're all high and mighty, just know that Ryan's infatuation with you is just a passing thing."

Angeline is still swaying back and forth but she looks tremendously pleased by what she has said to Danny and is waiting to see if her venom hits the mark.

I see red and I open my mouth to lay into Angeline, which I know will be useless because she's drunk. But Danny gives a small shake of her head and I hold my tongue. Instead, Danny just takes my hand and gives Angeline a polite smile. "Well, it's nice meeting you but I have to get going. I have work tomorrow."

Danny walks around Angeline and I, of course, eagerly follow. Angeline just stands there dumbstruck that she doesn't get a rise out of Danny. And really, she should know better than to try to dual wits with Danny. Danny would chew her up and spit her out if she had it in her to do so.

As we walk toward my car, our hands clasped and gently swinging back and forth, I'm silent.

"Is something wrong?" Danny asks.

"No. Actually, everything is just right. You're amazing you know. You completely charmed my friends and even though you had every right to punch Angeline in the face, you were polite to her. You are a class act, toots."

"I had fun tonight. Thank you for inviting me. I really like Mike and Carter. I can see why you are friends with them. Even Cameron was really nice."

"It was fun tonight. But you know what would be even more fun?"

"What's that?" she asks.

"Making out with you in my car when we get back to your place. You know, to see how foggy we can get the glass?"

"That does sounds like fun. Count me in."

By the time I walked her to her door, I couldn't see anything outside of my windows.

# CHAPTER TEN

## Danny

I think I might be on the verge of completely losing myself in Ryan. While our time alone has been like a fairy tale, I'm surprised how much fun I had the other night with Ryan and his friends. Everyone was really nice...well, with the exception of Angeline and that creepy teammate of Ryan's. I shudder when I think about the conversation I had with Reece Malone. He wasn't very subtle in making his moves. I had been standing by myself, sipping a beer when he had approached.

"It must be my lucky night, finding the most beautiful girl here all by herself," he had said with oily charm. I could tell he was drunk or high by the hazy look in his eyes and deliberate way he was trying to talk.

I smiled at him politely and took another sip of my beer. I've had to deal with my share of suggestive lines by drunks and I knew it was best not to even engage.

Swaying slightly while he peered at me, he stepped very close and I could smell the liquor on his breath. He leaned in and whispered in I'm sure what he thought was a super, sexy voice, "I have about twenty different ways I can make you scream."

Okay, that was beyond suggestive and he was clearly a complete slime ball. "Hey buddy, why don't you step back and give me a little space here."

He took a slight step back but he was still too close. He was looking at me like I was a piece of candy. "S'all cool," he drawled. "You're just so damn fine, and I can imagine the fun we'd have together."

Luckily, I was saved from having to reply when Ryan interjected himself into the conversation, coming to my rescue. I am forever grateful that Mike immediately pulled Reece away.

Yeah, the guy gave me the major creeps and I would be happy never having to see him again. Ryan had asked me if I had been upset by something Reece said, and I wasn't about to tell him about the pathetically lame pickup line. I didn't want Ryan to have any reason to go after him.

So, it's been a week since Ryan and I made up and it has been phenomenal. We haven't been able to see each other the last few days between work, school and hockey but we constantly text each other on the phone and every night we talk for a few hours until we are both so tired we are practically falling asleep with our phones pinned to our ears.

And last night...last night Ryan surprised me when he showed up at Helping Hands Ministry with a huge bouquet of Stargazer Lilies. They are my favorite and I knew instantly he must have asked Paula what flowers to buy for me. I rewarded him with a kiss full of nips and bites which had both of us groaning. It was quickly stopped when Maverick walked into the kitchen and caught us. After yelling at both of us, he put us to work in opposite places so we didn't even see each other until we got done. We both laughed hysterically at that.

Best of all was before we left, I got to introduce Ryan to Sarge, my only real friend other than Paula. Sarge is a grizzled, Marine Corps veteran that had served in the first

Gulf War. He had his left leg blown off by a roadside bomb and was medically discharged in 1992 after serving thirteen years.

Unable to get a job, and feeling general self-worthlessness, Sarge turned to alcohol to numb his pain. He didn't have a family to lose like my dad did so he said it was no surprise he ended up on the streets so quickly.

I met Sarge on the first day I went to Helping Hands to visit my dad. They had struck up a quick friendship and tried to keep each other on the straight and narrow path. My dad lost out but Sarge persevered. After successfully completing Helping Hands' rehab program, he went on to stay sober now for the past five years and now serves as a counselor at Helping Hands.

After my dad died, I continued my friendship with Sarge in addition to volunteering at the shelter. He was like a surrogate father to me and next to Paula, he was all I had in this world.

Ryan and Sarge hit it off grandly. That is, after Sarge warned Ryan that he could still kill with his bare hands and if he hurt me, he would never see the killing blow coming. Ryan swallowed hard and just said, "You don't have to worry about that, sir." And then they became fast friends.

I watched them as they talked. I was a little worried about Sarge. Age and the years of alcohol abuse were wearing on him. His dark face was heavily lined with wrinkles and I noticed his hair was mostly white now.

Before we left, I gave him a hard hug and then looked him square in the eye. "You're okay, right, Sarge?"

"Of course, I am. Why are you asking?"

"You just look a little tired to me and I want to make sure you're taking care of yourself.

He chuckled. "Quit worrying your pretty head about me. I'm fine."

I hugged him again and whispered, "I can't lose you too so you better be telling me the truth."

Sarge kissed me on the forehead and told me to get the

hell out of there. He shook Ryan's hand and we both left.

I snap out of the memory of last night and start getting dressed. Tonight, Paula and I are going to Ryan's opening season hockey game. I put on a pair of jeans and a long sleeved t-shirt. Then I put on one of Ryan's old hockey jerseys he gave me to wear. It smells like him and gives me an odd mix of lust and comfort.

My phone gives a little buzz and I look at it. It's a text from Ryan and I can't help the smile that spreads across my face. It seems like smiling is all I've been doing since Ryan and I became an item and that's alright by me. I read his text.

**Sitting in locker room getting dressed. Thinking about u.**

I quickly write back.

**Ironic. I'm getting dressed & thinking of u2.**

He is quick to respond.

**Mmmmm. Now I'm thinking about u getting dressed.**

Oh Lord, now I'm thinking about him thinking about me getting dressed and it does funny things to my stomach.

**LOL! Get ur head out of gutter and into game. See you later. Good luck.**

He doesn't text back so I put my phone down and finish getting ready.

We get to Matthews Arena and find our seats just as the Husky's take to the ice for warm up. Ryan gave me the tickets so he knows exactly where I am sitting which is just two rows off of the glass behind the Husky's bench.

I watch him hungrily as he skates around. He looks gorgeous in his uniform and about ten times larger than life. He doesn't have his helmet on yet so as he skates, the wind whips his long locks back, throwing his face in perfect relief. He hasn't shaved today and the stubble makes him look wild and dangerous.

The team leaves the ice after about ten minutes of

warm up drills and as I watch Ryan step into the tunnel, Paula nudges me with her shoulder. "Girl, you got it bad."

"What? What do I have bad?"

"Don't play stupid with me, Daniella Cross. You're in love with that boy."

I scoff. I might be falling for him but I'm not there yet. I've only known him for a little over a week. There's no way I am in love. And I tell Paula that.

She just says, "Mmmm. Hmmmm." And keeps a smug look on her face.

Soon, the lights dim and the arena thumps with loud rock music. The Husky's starting line-up is announced. When I hear, "And starting at center and team captain, give it up for Ryan Burnham" I get out of my chair and I am screaming probably the loudest in the arena.

After the game starts, I am glued to the action. I watch Ryan avidly when he is on the ice. He is focused and spot on. By the end of the first period, he has a goal and an assist. As he skates back to the bench after his last line change before the period ends, he looks to where I am sitting and smiles at me. Just that small acknowledgment...that he is thinking of me during the game...makes my heart start thumping. I look at Paula and all she says is, "Mmmm. Hmmmm."

At the end of the first period, Paula runs out to have a smoke and I go to the bathroom, then get us each some popcorn and drinks. I make it back to my seat before Paula does and I am happily sitting there munching my popcorn when someone sits down next to me. Thinking it's Paula, I turn to smile at her but am caught off guard to see Angeline sitting there.

She doesn't say anything but just appraises me coldly.

Finally I say, "Hi, Angeline."

She doesn't acknowledge my greeting but instead says, "You know...I didn't believe it at first when Cameron told me that Ryan was fucking you, but I guess I can see a certain wild appeal to you. You're different, that's for sure.

If you're into trailer trash that is."

I take a deep breath and count to ten to try to calm myself before I respond. I am well aware we are in public and I don't want this to escalate, but I also am not going to stand idly by while she insults me.

"Look, Angeline. You and Ryan were over long before I came into the picture so your beef shouldn't be with me. It should be with him. And for your information, I'm not fucking him...yet."

I see her eyes flash hot with anger and she leans into me so she can whisper. "You play out all the fantasies you want about a happily ever after with Ryan but just remember...you'll never fit into his world. He comes from the type of life you can only read about and it has no room for people like you. Trust me...he won't go the distance with you."

These words strike at me deep but before I can even think about what to say, I hear a tapping sound and we both turn to see Ryan standing there knocking his stick against the glass. The rest of the players are back on the ice warming up. He's staring at Angeline with murder in his eyes. She merely turns to me and says, "Think about it. You know I'm right."

I glance back to Ryan and I think he might crawl over the glass he's so mad. Then I hear, "Get out of my seat you, skanky bitch."

It's Paula and she makes an imposing figure in her shredded jeans, Motley Crue t-shirt and green military jacket. She's wearing heavy black eyeliner and black lipstick and even though she's diminutive, she looks tough as nails. I get a small measure of satisfaction when Angeline pales a bit and then scurries away.

I let out a breath I apparently had pent up and glance again at Ryan. He mouths the words *"Are you okay?"* to me and I nod my head with a smile. He looks at me for a few more seconds and then skates off.

Paula sits down. "What did she say to you? You're as

white as a ghost."

I'm quiet for a minute and then I look at her. "She basically said I wasn't good enough for Ryan. That our worlds are just too different to make it work."

"What the fuck, Danny? And I'll cough up my cigarette to you after the game. Why are you letting her get to you?"

"I don't know. She just sounded so genuine about our differences that it made me think twice about it."

"Well, you can get that out of your head right now. That boy is crazy about you and the both of you can make this work if you want it to. Now get those doubts out of your head."

I let out a shaky breath and mentally put my head back on straight. "You're right. Why am I even listening to her?"

"That's my girl."

I turn my attention back to the ice and let my thoughts focus on Ryan again. I'm so proud of him out there and at the end of the game, he comes over to the glass with a big grin on his face. They have won 3-2 and he is responsible for a goal and two assists. He pulls his helmet off and his hair is soaking wet. It's amazing he can look utterly gorgeous while being covered in sweat. He taps his stick to the glass and winks at me. I grin at him, my heart getting more deeply entrenched in all things Ryan Burnham. He nods his head to the right and I see he wants to meet me over at the railing to the tunnel that leads onto the ice.

Paula gives me a quick hug goodbye and says she'll see me at home later on. I pick up our garbage and throw it away, and then make my way over to the rail. I quickly climb over it and jump to the concrete.

Ryan is waiting for me and as I get closer to him, I appreciate just how enormously tall he is in his skates. I sure hope he's steady in them because just a few feet from him I launch myself into his arms and wrap my legs around his waist. He's wearing too much gear for my legs to wrap all the way around him but his hands are firmly gripping my ass to hold me in place. I plaster my mouth to his and he kisses me back with abandon, squeezing me tight.

I move my mouth to his neck and nibble there. "I'm so proud of you, Ryan."

He groans but says, "Danny...I'm all gross and sweaty."

"I don't care," I say as I work my way back to his mouth. After kissing him lightly there, I murmur against his lips, "I plan on getting sweaty with you a lot in the future."

Ryan whips around and crushes me to the wall with his body and thoroughly claims my lips with his. Eventually, he pulls back and I'm thankful no one has walked by us yet. "You know it makes me crazy in lust with you when you say things like that."

I smile coyly at him and stroke his face. "Ryan...what are we waiting for?" I know my eyes are full of yearning and I hope he understands the depth of it.

He looks at me deeply and then puts his forehead against mine. "Fuck if I know. Can I stay with you tonight?"

"God yes," I whisper and kiss him again.

# CHAPTER ELEVEN

## Ryan

Apparently, tonight's the night. I hope it's not happening too fast for Danny. It's certainly not happening too fast for me but I feel like a teenage boy getting ready to have sex for the first time. I'm apprehensive and excited all at the same time. And I don't mean horny excited, although I'm sure I'll get there. I'm excited to be with Danny in this way because then she'll be truly mine.

Danny opens the door to her apartment and we walk in. She flips on the lights and lays her purse down. I stand there with my hands in my pockets watching her. She turns and the look on her face is one of nervousness and it makes me doubt what we've set out to do tonight.

I walk to her and cup her cheek. She takes in a shaky breath and smiles at me tremulously.

"Ryan..." she whispers.

"Sshhh...we don't have to do this tonight," I assure her.

She gives a slight shake to her head, closing her eyes briefly. When she opens them back up, the anxiety is gone and in its place is desire. It makes my heart trip over and my body harden with anticipation.

"I was going to say that I want you so much it scares me," she murmurs as she reaches on her tip toes to place a soft kiss on my mouth. My eyes close and I inhale deeply. I clench the fist that's still hanging down by my hips, otherwise, I might grab her and throw her over my shoulder like a caveman. I let my breath out in shaky spurts.

# Danny

My entire body is trembling over the way Ryan is looking at me right now. With nothing more than a soft touch to my face, I'm already a hot mess of firing nerves. I want this so badly that the depth of my need scares me. If I could crawl into Ryan's skin right now, I would...just to be closer to him.

Ryan puts his hands on my hips and draws me closer to him. My hands go to his chest and curl into his shirt. He's wearing a light blue, button down shirt and dress pants since the players have to wear formal attire on game day. His jacket and tie are in his car, tossed haphazardly in the back. He smells of spicy body wash and I put my nose to his chest and inhale deeply.

"Danny?"

"Mmmmm?" My lips are to his chest so I can't give a more complete answer.

"Is this your first time?"

My cheeks flame a little red as I nod. "Am I that obvious?"

Ryan tucks his hand under my chin and draws my face up to look at him. "Not at all. I was merely hoping I'd be your first."

My mouth curves into a smile because the look he is giving me is one of possessiveness and craving. "It's the right time, Ryan. I want you to be my first...my only."

Ryan groans at my words and captures my mouth. It's

demanding and sweet all at the same time. Pulling back he looks at me, bringing his fingers to graze over my lips. "I'm a little nervous. We'll go slow because I don't want to hurt you."

I shake my head and giggle. "I'm a twenty-one year old virgin who has been fairly athletic most of her life. I doubt I have much of a hymen for you to shred."

Ryan chuckles as he swoops back down for a quick kiss before he pulls back. "Stay right here and then come back to your room in about five minutes, okay?"

I nod my head. He starts down my hall but then turns to look back. "Where's Paula?"

I shrug my shoulders. "She said she'd see me back here but she may have decided to be scarce. I think she knows I plan on seducing you tonight."

"Is that so?"

"That's so. Now hurry...your five minutes is ticking."

# Ryan

Danny is a virgin and she's chosen to give that sacred gift to me. I'm beyond honored and now ridiculously nervous all over again. I don't want to hurt her and I want to make sure I pleasure the hell out of her. The responsibility is heavy but I'm up to the task. Literally.

I get busy setting up her room. I turn on her lamp with the red scarf over it and turn the rest of the lights off. I pull out my iPhone and hook it to her alarm clock stereo. I scroll through my playlists, finally choosing some Jill Scott and turn it down enough so we can just hear the beat. Putting a condom on the bedside table, I sit on the edge of the bed and put my head in my hands. I want this to be so fucking perfect for her.

# Danny

I slowly open the door and my breath catches. Ryan is sitting on the bed with his head in his hands. I'm fearful that he is regretting this but then he looks up at me and my knees almost buckle from the heat in his eyes. They seem to be glowing like new pennies in the soft red light from my lamp.

He holds his hand out to me and I walk toward him. Locking his hand around my wrist, he pulls me forward until I'm standing between his legs. Placing a kiss on the palm of my hand, he releases it to wrap his arms around my waist and lays his head against my breasts. My arms automatically come up and wrap around his head, holding him tightly to me.

I don't know how long we stay like that but I tune into our mutual breathing which is slow and heavy. Finally, Ryan pulls his head back and looks at me. His hair flops boyishly over his forehead and is hanging over his eyes. I brush it back so I can see him.

"Danny, I'm falling in love with you. I just...need you to know that."

I smile at him and I can feel my eyes misting. "I'm already there. Glad you caught up."

I say those words without hesitation because the realization hits me overwhelmingly that I am hopelessly and completely in love with Ryan. And I could give a shit that we have known each other for only a week. There are no doubts for me. I may choose to regret the speed with which this is happening later in my life, but I won't regret it now.

# Ryan

My chest literally swells and expands to the point where

I think it might explode. Danny loves me? Danny loves me! And that realization makes me happier than any moment I can even remember in my entire life. About the closest thing I can compare it to is when I got recruited to play at Northeastern and even that feeling fizzles compared to this.

Standing from the bed, I hoist Danny up to my waist and her legs grip me tightly. I turn and kneel on the bed, taking her with me. Covering her body completely, I begin to kiss her. Long slow strokes, rimming the inside of her teeth, licking her lips, pulling on her tongue. She is moaning softly and her fingers are dug firmly into my shoulders. I want her to dig harder so I move down her throat, lightly sucking on her collarbone.

Danny turns her head to the side so her lips are near my ear and whispers, "More." She flexes her fingers into me a bit harder.

I pull away from her and kneel between her legs. Reaching down to cup the back of her head, I pull her into a sitting position and whip the jersey and her t-shirt over her head in one swift move. She's wearing a black bra made of lace and it looks sinful.

While I'm gripping the back of her head and gazing at her breasts, Danny reaches up and starts to unbutton my shirt.

# Danny

My hands are shaking with the need to touch Ryan's bare chest. I slowly work the buttons open and then peel the material back and off of his shoulders. He's wearing a plain white t-shirt underneath. I lean forward and place a kiss in the center of his chest, my lips burning from the heat coming off his skin and through the cotton material.

Ryan scoots off the bed and stands. He shrugs his dress shirt off and pulls his t-shirt over his head. Then he stands straight and undoes his belt buckle. My pulse freezes for a split second then it jackhammers into overdrive. Ryan is stripping in front of me. I'm all at once shy and hungry. Do I stare? Do I avert my eyes?

I opt for stare.

Ryan holds my eyes as he removes his belt. He toes his shoes off and bends quickly to remove his socks. Before going further, he reaches over and pulls my shoes and socks off, taking time to lightly run a finger of each instep. Goosebumps spread over my body and I try hard not to giggle. He grins mischievously at me before straightening back up.

And then his look turns serious as he starts to unzip his pants. I swallow hard but my mouth just waters again. My eyes can't help it but they leave his gaze and travel downward. Like a dream, he reveals himself slowly to me and I think he is the most beautiful creature I've ever seen. He's both hard and soft, soft and rough. The hard planes of his body synchronize perfectly with gentle curve of his biceps, his ass, his shoulder. I want to run my lips over every square inch.

I glance back up at him and I can see a muscle ticking in his jaw as he watches me shamelessly ogle him. I curve my mouth upward in a grin and he responds before he bends over the button of my jeans. I can't help but look down again at that hard part of him that will very soon be sunk deeply into me and I hunger for him.

# Ryan

My blood is pumping so hard through my body that I hope I don't have a coronary. When Danny's gaze travels from my eyes to my dick, I'm surprised I don't come right there by the way she's devouring me. My breathing increases and I feel like the earth tilts further on its axis.

I bend over Danny and work her jeans open. Her belly

button piercing glimmers in the soft light and I lightly run my tongue over it. She arches into me and I feel her hands lightly in my hair.

Pulling her jeans down, I see the briefest hint of the lacey black panties she's wearing and I swear I get harder. When her jeans hit the floor, I crawl up her body and settle between her legs. Her hands are back in my hair and we kiss again, both trying to savor the moment. But it doesn't take long before our tongues move fervently and a groan rumbles out of me when Danny moves her hips against mine.

Her hands are turning insistent, tugging on my hair, digging into my scalp. She may draw blood and I find I want her to. I love my sweet Danny but right now I want the part of her that's dyed and pierced to come through. She grinds her hips up against me and moans. Aaahh...there she is.

I rear back and roughly command her take off her bra. She sits up and does so without question, her eyes shimmering with lust. I grab the edges of her panties and pull them down her legs and fling them aside. Kneeling between her legs, I do nothing but just look at her. I let my eyes roam and feast, memorizing the path I intend for my lips to take.

I look to her navel.

Yes, I think I'll start there.

# Danny

Ryan bends over me and my breath hitches when he kisses my stomach. He runs his tongue over my piercing and his long hair falls to my stomach, tickling and burning me at the same time. I thread my fingers through his hair and sigh.

Then his tongue drags across my belly to my hip bone. He sucks hard and I gasp. His mouth becomes soft and he licks me like a bowl of cream.

Ryan moves everywhere below my stomach. Kisses to the inner most part of my thigh while his fingers dig into the globes of my ass. He's getting closer to that most intimate part of my body and I let out a husky shout when he finally makes contact. And then I'm spinning out of control.

My body is coiled tight like a snake about to strike and the pleasure is so overwhelming I feel like I'm going to burst into tears of joy. I'm on the edge and I want to fall. Unable to tell where his lips end and his tongue starts, Ryan murmurs against me, "Let go, Danny," and I take the plunge over the cliff. I can't help myself but I scream out and I think it's Ryan's name that falls from my lips but I can't be sure. My body is quaking, little shocks of pleasure still coursing through me. All I know is that I've just experienced the most physically intense sensation of my life and I've verified that I am indeed a screamer.

# Ryan

Danny tastes sweeter than I ever could have ever imagined and I can't imagine anything hotter than when she comes. I place a few more soft kisses on her belly and then I raise up. Her eyes are soft, shimmering. I reach over and grab the condom, opening the wrapper and tossing it aside. As I start to put it on, Danny reaches out and softly says, "Let me."

She takes the condom and my hands fall to the side. She's awkward and fumbling but my heart is lost to her over the fact that she wants to do this. When she first touches me, a low guttural sound erupts from my chest and I jerk in her hands. She gently finishes her task but she continues to stroke me and my eyes practically roll in the back of my head.

Pulling her hands away, I put them over her head and

hold them with one hand. I lay between her legs and press against her. As I lean down to her mouth, I whisper, "I love you" before plunging my tongue into her. She meets my desire and her legs fall further open. I slowly, gently rock into her while we continue to kiss.

Her breath is coming out in harsh pants and I move my head to her neck. I grit my teeth over the intense pleasure and with one more firm move of my hips, I'm fully seated. I pull up to look at her and her face is flushed with pleasure.

"Are you okay?"

She nods, her teeth holding on to her bottom lip, her eyes half closed.

And then we start to move.

Our hands are roaming as we both try to cover every inch of flesh that we can. My head moves to her breasts while her hands dig into my shoulders. I'm moving faster, harder within her and I feel a slow burn begin at the base of my spine. I'm not going to last much longer.

"Danny, I want you to come again," I pant with a particularly hard thrust.

She answers me with a small cry, and then her fingers dig into my shoulders as she comes apart. It's all over for me and I explode inside of her. I swear, my vision goes black for just a second, then Danny's beautiful face comes into clear focus.

My lust is completely spent but my heart is full. Danny's fingers skim lightly over my lips and she says, "That was fucking awesome." I bust out laughing and squeeze my girl to me, reveling in the feel of her skin against mine.

# CHAPTER TWELVE

## Danny

I bounce out of the shower the next morning, completely hyped up on post-coital bliss. Ryan's lovemaking was more than I had ever imagined and I am thinking about a million different dirty things that I want to do to him. Holy crap, I just made myself blush and I giggle to myself.

After I get dressed in a pair of yoga pants and t-shirt, I practically skip my way to the kitchen.

Paula is in there, leaning against the counter and drinking her coffee. She looks adorable with her face freshly scrubbed and wearing a pair of pink flannel pajamas with little yellow ducks over them.

I hop over next to her and plant a loud kiss on her cheek. "Good morning, my lovely roommate."

Paula groans. "You got laid last night, didn't you?"

I don't say anything for a minute as I pour myself a cup of coffee and lean against the counter opposite of her. After I take a small sip, I say, "More than once."

A slow grin comes to Paula's face. "Was it good?"

"Oh. Em. Gee. It was freakin' amazing. I never knew.

If I had known, I would have been doing this all along."

Paula snorts at me. "No you wouldn't because first, you're not that type of girl, and second, it's only amazing like that because you both are so sickly in love with each other."

"Really?"

"Really. Trust me."

I take another sip and then I give her a sobering look. I want her to understand I'm not kidding around right now. "He's it for me, Paula. He's my one and only."

Taking her last swallow of joe, Paula places her cup in the sink. She turns to look at me with her arms crossed. "You know I'm enough of a skeptic that I would tell you that is a young and idealistic way of looking at this relationship. But...I actually believe that he may be your one and only. I'm happy for you, kiddo. You deserve that type of love."

I put my cup down and grab Paula in a tight hug.

"I'm ready for it," I whisper. "I am so ready."

We squeeze each other for several seconds then release. Paula starts padding down the hallway. She calls back to me. "What do you have planned today? You and Ryan aren't going to be around here having wild monkey sex are you?"

"Nope. You're safe. Ryan said he'd be back in a few hours to take me on a picnic."

Paula makes a gagging sound but I see her smiling. "That's so fucking sweet my teeth hurt."

"That's two cigarettes you owe me," I remind her. "One from last night and one for just now."

✦

Paula is gone to work by the time Ryan shows to pick me up. I have been buzzing with nervous energy and I must have looked at my watch every thirty seconds.

It's unseasonably warm today for the first week of

October and I've decided to wear a long maxi-dress with a light cardigan over it. I put on a pair of white sandals and braid my hair into two long pigtails that follow the form of my neck and hang over my shoulders.

I open the door and Ryan runs his eyes down my body. I can see the appreciation over the low cut of the dress and the way you can just barely see the inside curve of my breasts. He looks back up and says, "Those pigtails are hot."

He steps in and pulls me to him hard and kisses the breath right out of me. His hips flex into mine and his desire is evident.

I have two choices. With a mere suggestion I'm sure I can get Ryan to take me into my room and make love to me, or I can do something I have been thinking about all day. I decide to go with the latter.

I break away from Ryan's kiss and start working the button to his jeans.

"What are you doing?" he asks in a sexy, growling way.

"Something I've been fantasizing about all day."

I hear his sharp intake of breath and I know he knows what I want to do. I finish undoing his pants and pull them down over his hips, dropping to my knees at the same time.

Ryan's hands lightly grip the side of my head but he is uncertain when he says, "Danny...are you sure?"

I don't answer but show him what I want to do. Ryan's breath hisses through his teeth and he bucks against my mouth, holding my head tight. "Fuck, Danny...please don't stop."

I have no intention of stopping, especially when I see how he completely and utterly unravels in front of me. I'm apparently pretty good at this because Ryan doesn't last long, shouting my name as he releases into me.

Hmmm...that might take some getting used to, but everything up until that point was mind blowing. I'm already calculating when I can do this to him again.

Ryan pulls me up by my shoulders and gives me a hard kiss. I know he can taste himself on my lips and I'm shocked beyond reason that he does this. But it also turns me on in a deep, dark way.

Finally pulling away from my kiss, Ryan says, "Let's go before my plans for a picnic get ruined by me taking you to your bedroom and screwing your brains out."

I snicker and hurry down the hall to brush my teeth before we leave.

◆

The park Ryan has taken me to is busy. The green fields are dotted with people just like us, taking advantage of a warm Boston day. We are able to find a spot that is away from the hustle and bustle of the numerous flag football and Frisbee games going on.

Ryan and I are laying side by side on a blanket. The only place we are touching is our pinky fingers which are hooked around each other. The sun is warm and bright. I'm full from our lunch and I feel lazy and in love. It's a wonderful combination and I highly recommend it.

Rolling over to my side, I put my head on my hand and look at Ryan. Running my fingertips along his jaw, his lips curve into a smile and he opens his eyes. He turns to his side, resting his head on his bicep and just stares at me.

"Tell me more about your family. You're unusually quiet about them," I say.

Ryan grabs my fingers that are skimming his face and kisses the tips. "What do you want to know?"

"Just...everything. Tell me what you want me to know."

He looks at me earnestly. "I want you to know everything about me."

I lean over and kiss his jaw. "So spill."

Ryan chuckles. "Well, I don't have the type of relationship with my parents that you had with yours. It's cold...almost sterile. There wasn't a lot of love or hugs in my household." He pauses a second. "I think that's why I love touching you so much."

My heart squeezes painfully thinking of the boy that didn't have hugs. I vow to myself that I will hug him every day for the rest of my life.

"Do you have any siblings?"

Ryan nods. "My younger sister, Emily. She's a senior in high school here in Boston."

"What's she like?" I'm thinking we can have girlfriend/sister shopping and lunch dates.

"She's a lot like Angeline. Spoiled, bratty, entitled. We aren't very close. My mother has had more of an influence on her than anyone."

Okay. I'll mark the girlfriend/sister lunch dates off my list.

I scoot over close to Ryan and lay my head on his chest, wrapping my arm around his waist. "I'm sorry you don't know what it's like to have a loving family. That must have been tough."

He shrugs his shoulders. "I guess. I'm close to my uncle...the one I told you played in the NHL. He's one that comes to all my games. He's the one that calls me to see how school is going."

"I'd like to meet him sometime," I murmur.

Ryan squeezes me. "I can't wait for him to meet you. He's going to adore you."

"Do you think I'll meet your parents anytime soon. I mean, you've met mine...Paula and Sarge that is."

Ryan releases me and pushes me back a little so I can see his face. He rubs his thumb over my cheekbone and has a sad look on his face. "Danny...my parents wouldn't like you. I am so ashamed to say that they will judge you because you look different than them and you don't come from money. They won't even bother trying to look at all of the amazing things that I see in you. And I'm so sorry for that because they'll never know what a fantastically amazing woman you are."

Ryan's words hurt me, not because of what they would think about me, but because they don't have the ability to care enough for their son the way parents should. I hate that his parents are so rigid in their ideals of what constitutes the right girlfriend for their son, that they would sacrifice his happiness.

"You deserve better than that, Ry."

"Ry? I like that." He kisses me softly then sits up on the blanket. He looks nervous and I sit up opposite of him, cocking my head slightly.

"I need a favor. I would like you to do something for me."

I smile indulgently at him. "Anything for you."

Ryan turns his back on me to reach into the gear bag he brought. He had our lunch packed in there along with a bottle of wine that we drank a few hours ago. I can't see what he's doing but when he pulls back from the bag and turns to me, my breath freezes in my lungs.

Held in his hands is a violin case. "Will you play for me?"

I look at him and his eyes are wary because he knows I would not want him buying anything for me. I clasp my hands in my lap and look down at them. The tears are filling up in my eyes and yet my fingers itch to take the instrument.

"Before you say no, Danny, please know that I need to give this to you. I need you to be complete and you can't be until you have music back in your life."

Oh, how those words affect me. Ryan is trying to make my life complete. What have I done to deserve that from him? I look up to him and a single tear falls down my cheek. He reaches out and wipes it away.

"Please let me do this for you," he begs.

I reach out and my hands are shaking as I take the case from him. I lay it gently on the blanket and pop the clasps to open it. Inside is a gleaming Bazzini violin. I rub my fingers lightly over the wood and look back at him.

"Thank you," I whisper. "It's beautiful."

"Play it for me," he demands softly.

Lifting the violin out of the case, I take measure of its size and weight. It feels strange in my hands and I feel an overwhelming sense of grief over the violin that I had sold a few months ago to help pay for my mom's medical expenses. I had had it since I was eleven years old and it was like losing an old friend.

I look into the case and there is a small pitch pipe. I pick it up and blow on the A note. I pluck the corresponding string on the violin and it rings true. I do each of the successive strings, only having to make a small tweak to each tuner.

Glancing at Ryan I see he is watching me intently. He gives me an encouraging smile.

I pick up the instrument and tuck it under my chin. I tighten the bow, draw it over the rosin and quickly run through the scales in each key. I'm rusty and awkward but I don't care. The simple notes coming out are beautiful in a way that only a music lover would appreciate.

Taking a deep breath, I close my eyes and I start playing *Mozart's Violin Concerto No. 5 in A*. The music is ingrained in me and the notes come out smoother and cleaner with every second that passes. I immerse myself in the sound, in the vibrations running through my hand, in the way the strings are cutting into my fingers because I've lost my callouses from lack of play. My heart swells with the music and I can feel tears leaking out of my eyes, but I keep playing. I don't want to stop, ever again.

After what could be minutes or hours, awareness of the outside world sweeps back in as I play out the last, long notes of the piece. I inhale shakily and let it come out slowly. And then I hear loud applause and my eyes spring open. Several people have gathered nearby and were listening to me play. I give them a small smile and then turn to look at Ryan.

He has a light sheen in his eyes and it's clear he is

deeply moved. I just stare at this incredible man who has given me back something that I honestly didn't think I would ever have again. And then I throw myself into his arms and kiss his face all over, whispering I Love You's with every touch of my lips. He takes the violin from my hands and sets it aside. Pushing me back down to the blanket, he rolls over on top of me, framing my face with his hands.

"Thank you," I whisper.

"My pleasure," he replies and kisses me again. When he pulls back, he grins wickedly at me. "You know, that was really hot. Think I can get you to play for me naked while you straddle me?"

I burst out laughing. "I think I can arrange something."

# CHAPTER THIRTEEN

## Ryan

The sun is streaming in through the window of my room and it's hitting Danny on the head, making it look like she's wearing a halo. She's so cute lying there...on her stomach...studying. She has a pencil gripped between her teeth and her brow is furrowed. I'm sitting at my desk, trying to get studying done of my own, but it's not working. I keep looking over at her and find myself getting lost.

I smile because apparently Danny has figured something out. Her scowl disappears, and one cute dimple peaks out. She erases something with her pencil and writes something else instead. She looks extremely satisfied with herself.

Oh, to hell with studying.

I stand up from my chair and walk over to my bed. Danny is deep in thought and doesn't pay any attention to me.

I'll change that.

I quickly cover her body with my own and hear her intake of breath before she giggles.

Pulling her long hair back away from her neck, I lightly graze my lips back and forth, just below her ear. She shivers in response and squirms underneath of me.

"Do you like that?" I ask softly in her ear, just before I lick the outer edge.

Danny issues a low groan and I flex my hips into her butt in response so she can feel what she's doing to me.

"Ryan...lock your door..."

I jump up from the bed to do her bidding but just as I reach the door it swings open. Mike is standing there with a shit-eating grin on his face. I glare at him.

"Hope I didn't interrupt anything?"

Danny laughs under her breath and I look back at her. She's flipped over and scooted back to lean up against the headboard. She's resting her head on her knees, looking completely innocent. I sigh and step back for Mike to come in, knowing that I'll have to wait to get my fill of Danny.

"What's up, man?" I ask.

"I come bearing bad news, buddy. Your mom is downstairs and wants to see you."

"Fuck!"

I scrub my hand through my hair in frustration. My mom has been trying to reach me for days and I've been ignoring her phone calls. I was hoping she'd just get tired of it and leave me alone. She is on a mission to try to get Angeline back in my life and that will happen when Hell freezes over.

I walk over to Danny and kiss her on the head. "I'll be right back."

Mike pipes up. "I'll keep her company while you go battle the grizzly bear."

"Thanks, dude."

I slowly trudge down the stairs, feeling like I'm walking to my death. My mother has a way of making me feel about two inches tall, just with a look. I will have to steel myself to tell her in no uncertain terms that I am not getting back with Angeline. In fact, now is as good a time as any to tell her about Danny.

As I enter the foyer, my anger burns. Angeline is standing there beside my mother. They're both dressed in their best. Wool and cashmere and thousands of dollars in pearls. I'd take Danny in a ratty t-shirt and sweat pants any day.

"Mother," I say as I walk up to her and bend over to give her a peck on the cheek. "What are you doing here?"

My mother appraises me closely and then practically sneers. "If you'd bother answering your phone or returning my calls, you'd know."

"Sorry. I've been busy with school and hockey."

She doesn't pull any punches when she says, "That's not all you've been busy with so I hear."

I glare over at Angeline who is smiling at me blandly. There's no doubt she's been filling my mother's head with all kinds of nonsense.

"I'm an adult, mother. What I do is none of your business."

She looks like she's going to lay into me for a minute but then changes her mind. Instead, she fixes a smile to her face and says breezily, "I don't want to fight with you, darling. I've come to take you to lunch and I invited Angeline along, too. Won't that be nice?"

My rage peaks again and is threatening to boil over. What do I have to do to get these two to see that I want nothing to do with Angeline?

"May I speak with you in private, Mother?" I say this through gritted teeth in an effort not to yell at her.

She inclines her head toward me to indicate she agrees, and I turn to walk back up the stairs. She follows without question.

I open the door to my room and Mike's head pops up. He's playing his PSP.

"Can you give us a minute, Mike?"

He jumps up from the bed and leaves the room,

mumbling a goodbye to my mother. I look at Danny and she looks like a deer caught in the headlights. She starts to get up from the bed but I hold my hand up to stop her. "Please stay."

I turn and step aside so my mother can walk in. She does so and inhales her breath sharply when she sees Danny sitting on my bed. Danny stands up, nervously wiping her hands on her jeans. I hate putting her in this position but I need my mother to understand what Danny means to me.

I walk over to where Danny is standing and put my arm around her waist. Leaning over, I give a small kiss to her temple and I feel her relax.

"Mother. This is Daniella Cross but she goes by Danny. Danny, this is my mother, Celia Burnham."

Danny reaches her hand out to my mother to shake it and good manners dictate that my mother has to reciprocate. "It's a pleasure, Mrs. Burnham."

My mother doesn't reply to Danny and releases her hand. Instead she looks at me. "I thought you said we were going to talk in private, Ryan?"

"I'm sorry, but what I want to say needs to be said in front of Danny and I want you to hear me so there is no misunderstanding. I am with Danny. She is with me. We love each other...deeply, and there isn't anything you can say or do that is going to change that. I'm asking you..." Ryan pauses and takes a deep breath, "no...I'm begging you to please accept this and for once, let me be happy with something of my own choosing."

For just a split second, I think I see something like understanding cross her face, but then it shuts down. Her veneer is back in place.

And then she actually laughs. "Ryan...don't be silly. You can't possibly think you have something to justify a long term relationship with this girl."

I feel Danny tense up next to me but I give her waist a small squeeze of reassurance. "Mother, I not only think it,

I know it. Now, either you can be happy for me, or not, but I am with Danny and nothing is going to change that."

My mother's lips peel back in a snarl and her next words are like ice in my veins. "Ryan Burnham...you have obligations to this family and I am not going to stand by while you throw away what could be a very promising future on some two-bit waitress. Now tell me you understand what I'm saying so we can be done with this foolishness."

I take a deep breath and offer up a prayer requesting patience. I look at my mother. Her beautiful visage is curled into an ugly scowl and her attitude makes it that much worse. I exhale and choose my next words very carefully.

"I understand what you are saying." I watch her visibly relax. "But I don't accept what you are saying. We are clearly at an impasse and until such time as you can accept Danny being with me, we have nothing more to talk about. I'd like you to leave now."

Danny lets out a small gasp beside me and I squeeze her again.

My mom turns to leave but not before landing her cold eyes on Danny. "I hope you're pleased with yourself, you little gold digging tramp. You've managed to alienate Ryan from his entire family."

Danny almost sags against me but I hold onto her tight.

"Leave, Mother." I grit out.

She flips me one last glare and leaves, slamming the door behind her.

Immediately I turn to Danny and pull her too me. She's shaking and I stroke her back to soothe her. I hear the door to my room open up and assume its Mike. I turn to ask him to give me a few more minutes but I'm incensed to see Angeline standing there.

"What the fuck do you want?" I snarl and Danny's head pops up to see Angeline standing in the doorway. She pulls out of my arms and walks over to the window, turning her back on us. I think she's seen all she wants to.

Turning back to Angeline I just point to the door for her to leave but she just glares at me. "How could you do that to your mother, Ryan? Choosing that—"

I don't let her get the word out. I lunge at her and grab her arm, probably a little more roughly than I intended, but I want to stop those vicious words from coming out. I push her out the door and slam it in her face. Leaning back against the frame, I can hear Angeline stomping down the stairs. I rub the spot between my eyes feeling a tremendous tension headache coming on.

Then Danny's soft hands are on my face. She's staring at me with such compassion that for a split second I want to break down and cry like a baby. Instead, I grab her head and kiss the hell out of her. Pulling her in close to me, I turn us around and push her into the door. I pin her body with mine, dragging her hands above her head. I thoroughly consume her mouth in my zeal to make sure she is really mine. I'm terrified she might leave me just to get away from the insaneness of my family.

Burying my face in her neck, I beg her, "I need to fuck you, Danny...please ...let me..."

She doesn't hesitate as she reaches down to the front of my pants and strokes me. "I need you too, Ryan. Now lock the door."

◆

Danny and I are lying on the bed, our skin slick with sweat. We're on our sides and I'm spooned up to her back. My heart rate is finally returning to normal after what must have been the wildest and hardest sex I've ever had and now I'm filled with regret.

"I'm sorry that was so rough," I say as I stroke her arm.

Danny flips over quickly and puts a fingertip over my lips. "Oh no you don't, Mister. That was outrageously awesome sex and you are not to feel bad about that in any way. In fact, I insist we do that more often."

I let out a huge sigh of relief and smile at her. "Thank God! I thought it was awesome too but I was just so wild for you. I'm not sure I really knew what I was doing."

She gives off that low, smoky laugh of hers that shoots lust straight through my body. "Oh, you knew what you were doing. And it was freakin' fantastic."

I wrap her in my arms and squeeze her. "I love you so much, Danny. Please don't ever leave me."

She's quiet for a minute then she says in a small voice, "I'm always afraid you'll leave me. That one day I won't be enough for you."

Needing to drown out her doubts, I lean over her and kiss her hard. She responds and our hands seek out the other's body, laying claim...branding. I make love to her again, slowly this time, whispering all of my feelings for her the entire time, making sure she understands that my dreams of the future can only come to fruition if she's by my side.

When Danny finally tumbles with me into oblivion, she's whispering to me that she loves me, too.

# CHAPTER FOURTEEN

## Danny

It's Saturday and I've pulled a double shift at Sally's. I'm so tired and my feet are killing me. I was supposed to go to a party tonight with Ryan but I begged off, telling him to spend some quality guy time with his friends. A night of relaxation with a good book is what I need.

It's almost 11:00 p.m. when I finish my shift. I'm just getting ready to walk out the door when I get a text. It's from Ryan.

**Didn't go to party. Sick. Just woke up. Think food poisoning. Can u come over?**

I don't hesitate when I fire off a quick text.

**Of course. Be there in 30 min with soup.**

I head back into the kitchen and get some chicken noodle soup and crackers to take with me. Putting cash in the register to cover it, I walk out the door and head over to Ryan's frat house.

When I'm about a block from his house, I remember that Ryan was supposed to meet Mike over at the party. Realizing that Ryan was probably too sick to let Mike know what was going on, I fire off a quick text to Mike to let him know why Ryan didn't show

**Ryan texted me he is sick. Won't make party. I'm on my way over there now. I'll take good care of him. :)**

I hit send and walk up the steps. The front door is open, as it usually always is. Walking in, I can't see anyone around. They are all probably at the party. I jog up the steps to Ryan's room and open the door.

The room is empty and I look around in confusion. His bed is perfectly made, which doesn't make sense. I walk over to it and see his iPhone on the nightstand. Setting the soup down, I pick his phone up and turn it on. There are his texts to me and my responses. Maybe he's in the bathroom.

My phone chimes and I look down to see a text from Mike.

**Ryan's here with me. R U okay?**

A sick feeling begins in my stomach and before I can reply, something hard slams into the back my head. I crumple to Ryan's bed and my vision winks in and out. Someone grabs my hair from behind and pushes me face down onto the mattress, then a pillowcase is thrown over my head and I am now in full blown panic. I try to scream but only a warbled sound comes out. I take a deep breath and try again, getting out a somewhat loud shriek.

I'm rewarded with another hit to my head, this time to the side of my face and it catches the corner of my eye and my cheekbone. Pain explodes and fear for my life is now coursing through me. I'm dizzy from the blows to my head. I'm suffocating from the pillowcase pulled tight over my face and the weight of someone on my back.

And then my worst nightmares come true. Whoever is at my back reaches to my front and undoes my jeans quicker than I can react. I start struggling with all my might but my captor now has put a large hand around the back of my neck, pinning my face into the mattress. I can't breathe and I know I'm going to pass out.

I can feel my jeans and underwear being roughly jerked down my legs and cold air hits my bottom. I start thrashing again, trying to get free and my attacker pushes my face harder in the mattress and says, "Quit moving, bitch, and I'll make this fast."

Terrified, I start crying and I'm tiring out from the struggle. I'm weakly flailing my legs but he just laughs at my efforts. I feel one of hands his reach roughly between my legs and I start sobbing uncontrollably.

And then he's gone...as if he's been ripped away from my body. I hear Ryan bellow in rage and scream, "Get the fuck away from her." Something slams into the opposite wall.

I scramble to pull up my jeans and jerk the pillowcase off my head. Ryan is on top of a guy...I can't tell who it is. Ryan is pounding away at his face, over and over again. Blood and spit starts flying and I can see numerous cuts opening up on my attacker's face. I'm frozen in place, watching Ryan punch the man over and over.

Feet come running up the stairs and Mike is in the doorway. He flicks a glance at me, appraising the situation and mutters, "Fuck." He looks over at Ryan and just watches as he pounds away at my would-be-rapist. I hear the crunch of bone on bone and when Ryan pulls his fist back, I can see the guys nose squashed to the side of his face.

Finally, Mike moves in and tries to pull Ryan off. Ryan whips around on Mike, rage turning his beautiful face into a mask of hatred and vengeance. He snarls, "Get the fuck off me," and goes back to pounding on the guy, who is now unconscious.

"Ryan, you're going to kill the guy if you don't stop."

He doesn't listen and his rage isn't diminishing. I start crying, strangely sick at the gruesome scene before me and oddly satisfied that Ryan is hurting this guy who came so very close to killing a part of me.

Mike is yelling now and trying to grab Ryan again.

"Ryan...do you want to go to prison? Get off of him. He's done."

Mike's words do nothing to affect Ryan but when he says the word "prison" it jolts me into action. I can't have Ryan go to prison because of me.

I jump off the bed and cross the room in two strides coming to stand in his line of vision.

"Ryan," I say softly. "Please stop."

And just like that Ryan stops and stands up from the guy. He is breathing harshly and his hands are covered in blood. More blood is spattered on his shirt. He turns my way and runs his gaze over me. He stares at my face and with a shaky hand, he gently brings it up to touch where I can feel my cheek starting to swell. But then he must see the blood all over his hand and drops it back down to his side.

He looks lost and my heart breaks. I walk up to him and put my head on his chest. I wrap my arms around his waist and squeeze him hard. He doesn't respond at first and I start to panic. But then his arms come around me and he buries his head in my neck. I can feel him starting to shudder but then he pulls back abruptly.

"Are you okay?"

I nod, on the verge of a full meltdown.

"Did he...?"

"No! He didn't get a chance. He just...touched me."

Oh God, he touched me. I can feel bile rising in my throat and run to the wastebasket. I make it in time and heave and heave until nothing more is left. I'm dimly aware of Ryan cradling me in his lap, stroking my hair, telling me it's going to be alright.

✦

The police and rescue squad are here. They've taken my attacker away. It turns out it was Ryan's teammate, Reece Malone. He was unconscious and badly beaten. I'm terrified he might die and Ryan could be in serious trouble.

Ryan and I are both sitting in the back of an ambulance. An EMT is bandaging Ryan's hands and another is taking my vitals. I glance out the back doors and there is a huge crowd gathering. Ryan reaches across the space and links his fingers with mine. I squeeze back.

The EMT is asking me questions and I try to focus. She's asking me if I need a rape kit and I can feel my bottom lip trembling as I shake my head no. She questions me about my injuries and I tell her about being dizzy and vomiting. She's afraid I may have a head injury and wants me to go to the hospital to get checked out. She said they'll also need to physically document my injuries for any criminal charges.

I look over at Ryan in panic and he strokes his thumb lovingly over my hand. "It'll be okay, Danny. We need to take you to the hospital to get checked out."

I nod, trusting in Ryan.

At the hospital, they triage me fairly quickly and whisk me away for a CT scan of my head. Then they put me in a room where Ryan is waiting and I crawl onto his lap so he can hold me. The room we are in is depressing as hell. The walls are a dingy gray and are covered with old posters depicting different types of injuries. The smell of antiseptic is making me nauseous.

As we are waiting for a doctor, a police officer comes to take my statement and he takes photos of my bruises. Apparently there is a long scratch across my lower back that I don't recall how I got, but he snaps a few pictures of it. I'm beyond humiliated.

Before leaving, he tells us that he has to keep Ryan's cell phone for evidence, as it appears that Reece used it to lure me to the frat house by posing as Ryan, texting me that he was sick.

"I forgot to bring my phone with me to the party," Ryan murmurs. "Thank God you texted Mike. Otherwise...I wouldn't have known you were in trouble."

I shudder as I consider the probability of what would have happened had I not sent that text and Ryan hugs me tight.

As soon as the one cop leaves, another comes in.

"She's already given a statement," Ryan growls. "Can't you guys leave her alone?"

The officer looks at me with sympathy but then turns hard eyes to Ryan. "I'm not here to take her statement. I'm here to place you under arrest for assault and battery."

"What?!" I shriek a little too loudly and fly off of Ryan's lap. "He was defending me. You need to arrest that animal who attacked me."

"Ma'am. You need to calm down. We will press charges against Mr. Malone but he is asking that we press charges against Mr. Burnham."

"It's not fair," I whisper, and the tears start flowing again. Ryan gathers me in his arms and kisses my forehead. He asks the cop, "Can you wait until at least she sees the doctor so I can stay with her?"

The cop looks back and forth between us and then sighs. "Sure. I'll be outside waiting for you."

Before he steps outside he turns to look at us. "For what it's worth, if that had been my wife or my daughter, I would have done exactly what you did, Mr. Burnham."

Ryan nods at the cop who leaves and softly shuts the door behind him. Then he picks me up and sits back down, cradling me in his lap. "It's going to okay, Danny. Please don't worry."

I'm clutching his shirt while I lay my head in the crook of his neck. "How can I not worry? You're getting arrested."

"Sssshhh," he says. "Just close your eyes until the doctor gets here."

I do as he asks and then I melt when Ryan starts humming a song to me. I don't recognize it at first but then I realize its John Lennon's *Imagine*, one of my all-time favorite songs. I utterly sink into Ryan and let him sing to me to wash away my fears.

Eventually, Sarge arrives. I had called Paula at work and she was trying to find someone to cover her shift so she could come to me. Sarge was my next call after Paula. He hugs me and then puts Ryan in a big, bear hug, thanking him for saving me.

Finally the doctor comes and clears me. He says my CT scan is negative and that I should be just fine.

After he leaves, I turn to Ryan. Any words I want to say are stuck in the dryness of my throat. He asks for my phone and I hand it to him. He enters something in my contacts and hands it back to me.

"Please call my uncle tonight," he says. "I programmed it under Jim Thorne. He knows who you are. Tell him what happened and ask if he can arrange for an attorney for me. Ask him not to call my parents. I don't feel like dealing with them."

I nod then hug him hard. "I love you. More than anything."

"I love you too." He pulls back and kisses me on the temple. "Don't worry. I promise it'll be okay."

I start to walk out the door with him but he shakes his head no. "I don't want you to see me get arrested."

I nod as tears stream down my face, and the door closes behind him. Sarge takes me in his arms and hugs me again.

# CHAPTER FIFTEEN

## Ryan

I'm at my arraignment hearing the day after my arrest. Uncle Jim brought me one of my suits to wear and he's sitting with Danny behind me. I glance back at her and give her a reassuring smile. She returns it and mouths *I love you.*

Uncle Jim hired me a really good lawyer and he has prepared me that the judge will probably not throw the charges out at this point, but that I should be able to make bail with no problems. This satisfies me.

I know I should be afraid at the prospect of getting convicted but I'm not. And I have no regrets for beating that shit the way I did. I'd do it again if he even looks at Danny the wrong way. The only solace I have right now is that he is in jail for attempted rape and will most likely not make bail.

The hearing is short. I stand as the judge reads the charges against me and asks how I plead. I want to say, "I'd do it all over again, Your Honor" but instead I say, "Not Guilty" as my attorney instructed me to do. Bail is set at $10,000 which is easy money and then the hearing is over.

My attorney tells Uncle Jim and Danny that he'll walk me through the process of paying the bail and getting me released, and that we will meet them on the front steps of the courthouse.

✦

I walk out of the courthouse and immediately loosen the tie around my throat. I've always felt too confined in them. I glance around looking for Danny and Uncle Jim and when I find her my blood starts to boil. My mother is standing there and she and Uncle Jim are arguing. Danny is pale looking.

I jog over to them and as I come up behind my mother, I hear her say, "Well, he wouldn't be in this mess if it wasn't for her. Girls like her bring this stuff upon themselves."

"Celia!" My uncle says with warning. "That's enough."

I brush past my mother and gather Danny in my arms. I give her a hug and kiss her on her forehead. I pull back and look at her. She gives me a shaky smile.

Turning to my mother, I say the words that need to be said. "Mother, you've said the last hurtful thing about Danny that I will tolerate. I'm done with you. Do not contact me or reach out to me again. In fact, how about you just pretend I never existed."

Danny and my mother both gasp out loud.

"Ryan," my mother pleads. "You don't mean that. You can't choose her over your family."

I feel Danny flinch in my arms over those words. I look at my mom levelly. "Listen carefully, Mother, because I mean this with every fiber of my being. I am choosing love. I am choosing someone who loves me unconditionally, no matter what. It's as simple as that."

I turn and walk away, pulling Danny along with me. I can hear my mother crying and I even hear Uncle Jim say,

"You brought it upon yourself, Celia."

We walk to my Range Rover that Danny had driven today. She hands me the keys and I open the door to let her in. Before she steps in, I stop her and she looks at me. She has purple bruising over her right cheekbone. I reach my fingers out and skim over it gently. She closes her eyes at the touch.

I smooth my fingers into her hair and slide them to the back of her head. I need her so badly. I need to know none of this is scaring her away from me. Pulling her face toward mine, I tentatively touch my lips to hers. She sighs into me and lets herself go, entwining her tongue around mine. Relief courses through me as I realize I've not lost her.

✦

We are lying in Danny's bed, naked, and thoroughly replete. I'm on my back and she's lying on top of me with her head on my chest. I'm stroking her hair and her back, both feeling like silk under my palm.

Our lovemaking was slow and tender. When we got to her apartment, Danny's first words were, "Touch me, please. Make me forget."

And I did.

"What are you thinking?" Danny asks me.

"I'm actually thinking of your music. Can you get back into Julliard?"

Danny is quiet but then she answers softly. "I believe so. My audition was really good. And I withdrew for hardship reasons so I shouldn't have a problem."

"I think you should go back."

Her body stiffens in my arms and the lazy circles she was drawing on my chest with her fingers still.

"I can't afford it right now."

I sit up and pull her up with me. Holding her by the shoulders, I say, "Then let me help you."

Danny's shaking her head back and forth.

"Why not?" I demand.

My tone is harsh and I've never spoken to her this way before. She's taken aback for only a few seconds before her eyes go green on me with anger.

"Because I'm not some whore who takes gifts in return for sex. I already have enough of your friends calling me that...I don't need any more."

My mouth hangs open. "Is that what you think I'm doing? Paying you for sex?"

She doesn't say anything but won't meet my eyes. I gently take hold of her chin and make her meet my gaze. "Danny...I love you. I want to help you achieve your dreams. That's what people in love do for each other."

Danny deflates right in front of me and crawls onto my lap. "I know, and I'm sorry I'm such a bitch about this. It just seems weird to me. And I'm sensitive about how others view me. Your mom thinks I'm a gold digging tramp, remember?"

I'm quiet for a minute as I'm stroking her hair. Then I venture, "Would you feel different if we were married?"

She snaps her head up so hard it catches me on my chin with a resounding crack.

"Ouch," she swears.

I start laughing and rub the top of her head although I feel like I've been hit in the chin with a metal pipe.

Snuggling back to my chest, she softly says, "Don't joke about things like that. It's not funny."

"Who says I'm joking?"

She leans back to look at me once again, more carefully this time so we don't bang heads. Her eyes are wide and incredulous. "Ryan, we've known each other for like two seconds. How can you even think about marriage?"

Taking Danny's hands in mind, I look her dead in the eyes. "I can think it because I know, Danny. You're my one and only. Just like I'm yours. You know it's true."

She smiles and then kisses me. She doesn't respond and

moves her mouth to the area below my ear. She's trying to distract me but I'm not going to let it go. I'll just have to keep working on her until she either accepts my offer to help her with school or she agrees to marry me and then all of my money will be hers as well.

For now, Danny pushes me back down onto the bed and straddles me. As she rises up, I get lost in the perfection that hovers above me. We'll discuss school and marriage later.

◆

The next morning, I get up early and cook Danny breakfast while she sleeps. We have a big day because Malone's arraignment is today and she wants to be present. And there's no way I'm letting her go alone.

Then I have to go see Coach and fill him in on everything. Given the criminal charges against me, I'm fully prepared to lose my Captaincy. Hell, I may get tossed off the team. Again, I still can't have a single regret for what I did.

I'm flipping pancakes when Paula walks in. Her hair is sticking up all over the place and she's rubbing her eyes.

"G'mornin'," she mumbles. "Danny still sleeping?"

"Good morning, sunshine. How many pancakes do you want? And yes, Sleeping Beauty is still...well...sleeping."

Paula holds up two fingers to indicate her pancake preference and pours herself a cup of coffee.

"How's she doing?" she asks me quietly.

"She's okay. Her face is a little sore but she's otherwise doing fine."

I finish Paula's pancakes for her and hand her the plate. I turn the stove off.

"Can I ask you something?"

Paula looks at me while stuffing a fork full into her mouth then nods.

"I offered to help Danny go back to Julliard, but she won't let me. So I offered her marriage, and she looked at me like I was crazy. What in the hell am I doing wrong?"

Paula looks at me like I am the biggest dumbass on the face of the earth. She swallows her food and takes a sip of coffee. "Seriously, Ryan. You're such a dumbass."

*See, what'd I tell you?*

"What is so wrong with me wanting to help her fulfill her dreams?" I sound petulant but I can't help it. I don't see how I can be wrong about this.

"Listen up and listen hard. I'm going to give you the best advice you've ever had." She pauses for dramatic effect, and then says, "Wait."

I anticipate more pearls of wisdom but none are forthcoming.

"That's it? Just 'wait'?"

Paula nods.

"And that's really the best advice I've ever had?"

"You can thank me at any time." She grins at me.

I sigh. "Please expound just a little bit more. My brain is apparently not comprehending you right now."

Paula pushes her plate back and picks up her mug of coffee. Sitting back in her seat, she looks at me with a smile. "You're a good man, Ryan. All you need to do is give our Danny some time and she'll come around. She's been through a lot lately. I'm telling you, just give her time and let your offers sink in. My girl is no dummy. She'll meet you halfway, I guarantee it."

The pressure in my chest eases up and I smile fully at Paula. "Thanks. That makes me feel a ton better."

"What makes you feel a ton better?" Danny asks as she pads into the kitchen, her eyes heavy with sleep.

Her hair is a knotted mess, probably due to our activities last night. She walks up to me and crawls onto my lap. I rub my nose along the side of hers and say, "Oh, nothing. Paula was giving me a home remedy for some heartburn I've been having."

Danny yawns and snuggles into me. "That's nice," she says sleepily.

I look over the top of her head at Paula who gives me a conspiratorial wink.

I wink back and hug my girl.

# CHAPTER SIXTEEN

## Danny

The arraignment hearing is over and it couldn't have gone any better. Reece pled not guilty but was denied bail. It was painful sitting in the same room as him. I couldn't not help but think about how close he came to destroying me. I shudder imagining it and Ryan squeezes my hand.

Ryan sure did a number on him. His nose is in a splint and the district attorney said he has to have surgery on it. The rest of his face is covered with cuts and bruises. I glance at Ryan and he is glaring daggers at Reece.

After Court, Ryan drops Paula and me back at my apartment. He has a class to go to and then hockey practice. I have a shift at the diner. We make plans for him to come over to my place tonight after I get off work.

The dinner rush finally slows down around 7:30 p.m. and I pour myself a glass of ice water. Sipping at it, I watch as the door to the diner opens and in walks Ryan's mom. There is a young girl with her that has the same dark hair and whiskey eyes as Ryan. It must be his sister, Emily. She wears the same scowl as her mother.

My heart starts a mad thump in my chest. She's looking

straight at me and there's no doubt that she has come here to talk to me. I watch with trepidation as she walks up to the counter and inclines her head at me.

"Danny, would you be willing to talk to me?"

I nod my head, terrified of what she's going to say. I want nothing to do with this woman but I can't be sure she isn't here to try to patch things up with Ryan. And I would very much like them to make up.

I lead them over to a booth at the back of the diner. Celia doesn't bother to introduce me to his sister.

We sit down in the booth, Ryan's family on one side and me on the other. How apropos.

I look expectantly at Celia to say something. She doesn't mince any words. "It's no secret that I don't want Ryan seeing you. He clearly will not listen to me or see reason. So I need you to break things off with him."

Astounded, all I can do is stare at her. Does she think I'm just going to jump to do her bidding?

"I'm sorry, Mrs. Burnham, but you are sadly mistaken if you think I'm going to walk away from Ryan."

I watch as she leans over into her purse and pulls out a checkbook. She looks me straight in the eye and asks, "What is it going to cost me?"

Laughter bubbles up from my mouth and I can't hold it in. I know it's rude but I can't help it. This woman is trying to buy me off and the absurdity of it tickles me. She, on the other hand, doesn't see the humor and just waits for me to respond.

Finally, I remove the smile from my face and look at her solemnly. "There is no amount, Mrs. Burnham. I don't need or want your money."

She scoffs. "Nonsense. Everyone needs money."

I shake my head. "I don't. Now, if you'll excuse me..."

"Isn't it obvious, Mother?" Emily drawls.

My gaze snaps to her and I wait to see what she says.

"She's going to decline your money because she thinks Ryan is a bigger gravy train. She's in it for the long haul."

If I could reach across the table and throttle Ryan's sister, I would do it in a heartbeat. I remain calm though and stand up from the booth. I look down at them. "I'm sorry your trip here was wasted. Now I have to get back to work."

I turn to walk away but then Mrs. Burnham calls out softly. "Ryan is going to be ruined, you know?"

I'm not sure if this is a ploy but I turn my attention back to her. She merely points her finger at the seat I had just vacated and I sigh as I sit back down.

"I can make Ryan's criminal charges go away. My attorney has had contact with Mr. Malone's attorney, and we can offer him a very nice settlement in return for him dropping the charges against Ryan."

My eyebrows raise and now she has my complete attention. "That's wonderful," I say with excitement.

"Yes, I suppose it is," she says dryly. "But I'm not going to waste my money on this deal if Ryan is still with you. If you want me to bail Ryan out of this mess, you will break up with him and get out of his life for good."

My heart sinks to my stomach and turns into a lead weight. The solution to Ryan's criminal charges lie with this woman, and the price is steep. She wants me to give up the one thing in my life that represents a lifetime of love and happiness.

I try to call her bluff. "You wouldn't abandon Ryan like that."

She arches a perfectly plucked eyebrow at me. "Wouldn't I? He's already turned his back on our family, why wouldn't I do the same thing?"

I suck in my breath. How could the woman that birthed such a wonderful man as Ryan do this to him? Having had the most loving and wonderful mother in the world, it's just beyond my comprehension.

I bite at my lip and glance out the window at the darkened street. It was only ten short days ago that Ryan walked into my life...right here in this very diner. And now,

I am being asked to make a decision to give it all up. I've sadly come full circle.

Mrs. Burnham leans across the table. "Look...I can see you're a nice enough girl. But you could be his downfall. If he gets convicted, he can kiss a hockey career goodbye. Without my support in getting these charges dropped, Ryan could end up in prison. Do you want that to be on your head?"

My shoulders slump in defeat. What she is offering is the only sure way to get Ryan out of trouble. Trouble he would not have been in had he never even met me.

Celia leans forward and her look is coldly masterful. "Let me also make this clear. If you see Ryan or talk to him after the charges are dropped, I will personally see to it that he doesn't get into the NIIL. My husband has enough contacts that can kill any chances of him having this hockey career that he so very much desires."

This woman is a monster but I do nothing more than give a small nod of my head in agreement to her demands.

"Excellent. I expect you to break things off with him immediately."

She stands from the booth and Emily crawls out behind her. I keep my eyes down on the Formica table until they leave. Then I let the tears flow.

✦

Ryan is due at my apartment any minute and I'm trying to compose myself in a way that will make this breakup believable. I've asked Paula to make herself scarce tonight. She wants to know what is going on and I tell her I'll fill her in later. I'm sure her shoulders will be soggy by the time she gets me under control.

There's a knock at my door and my heart feels shredded already. I probably have less than five minutes left of having Ryan in my life. This is the same pain I felt when I lost my mother and I never thought I would feel this way again.

I open the door and Ryan steps in. He wraps his arms around me and buries his nose in my hair. I cling to him tightly for a moment and then step away. Staying in his arms any longer could be disastrous for what I need to do.

Ryan starts jabbering about practice but I'm only catching about every fourth word. I'm too preoccupied with how to launch into my speech.

"Are you okay, Danny? Have you heard a word I've said?"

He's looking at me with a soft smile on his face and his head is angled in curiosity.

"I'm sorry. What did you say?"

"I said the school is letting me stay on the team until we have resolution on the criminal charges. Even better, the entire team voted to have me remain as Captain. They're really rallying around us."

He takes me in his arms again and kisses me. His enthusiasm is infectious and I let it sweep me away for a few minutes. I want to have more memories of him so I will take these kisses as payment for the evil job I'm getting ready to do.

My body is eagerly responding to Ryan and I know if I don't back away, we are going to end up in bed together. And I most certainly cannot let that happen. There's no way I'll survive a goodbye fuck with the man I love.

I step back from Ryan and walk over to the couch.

"Ry...can we talk for a few minutes?"

I'm wringing my hands as I take a seat and the look on Ryan's face is cautious. He sits beside me and leans back, placing one arm on the back of the couch. I turn sideways so I can look him in the face.

I owe it to him to look him in the face when I break his heart.

Ryan skims my hair with gentle fingertips and tucks it behind my ear. I relish his touch. "What's wrong, baby? You're starting to worry me."

I reach out and grasp his hand and squeeze it tightly in mine. The tears pool in my eyes and I take a steadying breath.

"Ryan...I can't see you anymore." I look at him and I can tell he doesn't comprehend. "I can't be with you anymore. I want to break up."

Ryan pushes forward on the couch and frames my face with his hands so I'm focused on him. "Tell me this is a joke."

I shake my head, lowering my eyes. I can't stand the sorrow on his face. "It's not."

"Why?" he demands.

I start crying in earnest. How do I say words that aren't true but are guaranteed to slice deeply into his heart?

"I can't handle any of this..." I say vaguely.

"You'll have to be more specific, Danny," he grits out.

Ryan's face is awash in anger and disbelief. My stomach is rolling and my head is pounding. He's going to make me irrevocably hurt him.

I stand up and straighten my spine. I dash my tears away and look at him with as much disgust as I can muster. "You bring too much misery and chaos to my life, Ryan. Your parents hate me. Your friends think I'm a whore."

"But we've talked about this. We're handling those things together. I don't believe those things are driving you away from me."

I have to make the final push so he believes me. My soul dies over my next words. "For God's sake, Ryan...I almost got raped because of some pissing contest you had with your teammate. It's your fault."

Ryan's face blanches and so much pain fills his eyes that I think I might vomit. He's so wounded right now and I am the one that did this to him. My heart shrivels and dies. I'll never be able to forgive myself.

Ryan looks down at the carpet, confusion on his face. Then he looks back up at me.

"I'm sorry," he says quietly. "I didn't mean to cause you any pain."

Oh my God. I'm getting ready to lose it in front of him and I need him to leave before I break down and confess his mother's wicked plot. I reach on the other side of the couch and pull out my violin case. I walk to the door and open it. "Please leave, Ryan and don't contact me again."

I'm looking at the floor, trying to stop the flood of tears I can feel coming. Ryan walks up to me and I can feel him staring at me hard. I hold the case out. "Take the violin. I don't want it."

He doesn't say anything for a minute and I refuse to look at him. Finally, he says, "It was a gift to you, Danny. Throw it away if you don't want it."

Then he steps out the door and out of my life.

I softly close the door behind him and then sink to the floor, weeping for the torment I caused him.

# CHAPTER SEVENTEEN

## Ryan

I'm driving to my parents' home in Beacon Hill. My father is still in Washington, D.C. but my mother invited me to lunch. I am furious with her. I cannot prove it but I just know that she is behind Danny's sudden break up with me.

At first, when I left Danny's apartment, I was shell shocked. Everything that made me happy had suddenly been stripped from me. I was mad at Danny for all of about two minutes, but while I was driving back home, it struck me. Danny didn't have it in her to break up like that. On top of that, I know without a doubt that Danny loves me. It would take something monumentally sinister to get her to do that. And the most monumentally sinister thing I knew was my mother.

I've tried calling Danny several times. She won't answer the phone or return my messages. I've called Paula but she is vague and non-committal. She says she'll pass my messages on but I have no clue if she is really doing it. I've even staked out Helping Hands Ministry and Sally's, hoping to catch her so we can talk. She's avoiding me like the plague.

Now it's been two weeks since Danny booted me out of her life and I want answers. The formal criminal charges against me were dropped. My attorney worked a deal out with Malone's attorney. He may get a nominal part of my trust fund, but it's worth it not to have that shit hanging over my head. This news should make me deliriously happy but it tastes cold and bitter. None of it matters if Danny is not in my life.

I pull into the driveway and take a few meditative breaths. I'm going to need all the help I can get dealing with my mother.

Walking into the house, I hear voices coming from the back sunroom. I walk in and immediately spot Angeline sitting next to my mother. They stop talking when they see me and in the next instant, Angeline runs to me, throwing herself against my body.

"I've missed you so much, Ryan."

My arms remain at my side and I clench and unclench my fists in an effort to remain calm. When Angeline doesn't take the hint that I'm not returning her embrace, I peel her off of my body and step away from her.

"What are you doing here, Angeline?" My voice is cold and flat.

The smile drops from her face and she looks at my mother for help.

"I just assumed you'd be happy to see me now that you've broken up with that..." Angeline trails off when she sees the murderous look on my face.

"I invited her to lunch with us, Ryan," my mother interrupts. "Now stop being so rude."

I turn to Angeline. "You need to leave. And please accept my word when I tell you that I am not interested in you anymore nor will I ever be."

"Ryan!" my mother admonishes me.

Angeline doesn't move and she's looking back and forth between the two of us.

"Leave, Angeline. Now!" My voice is cold and furious, and she knows better than to test me right now. She scurries away like a small rodent and moments later I hear the front door slam.

My mother is looking at me with shrewd eyes. I take the seat that Angeline just vacated. "We need to talk, Mother."

Clasping the pearls around her neck, my mother leans back in her chair and crosses her legs. She can't help herself when she says, "Honestly, Ryan. I have no idea what's gotten into you. You are going to have to do some groveling now to get Angeline back."

I sit forward in my chair and rest my elbows on my knees, clasping my hands together. I look my mother straight into her eyes, and ask, "Do you ever really listen to anything I say?"

She looks confused. "What? Of course I do."

"Then one more time...I am not going to be with Angeline...ever again. So stop shoving her down my throat. You're doing nothing more than hurting her because you build up her expectations and I'm tearing them down. Just give it a break."

My mother swallows hard but her voice is firm. "Fine. I hear you. I'll stop throwing Angeline at you. No matter. There are plenty of acceptable women in this area."

I can feel my control slipping so I take another deep breath and exhale it out slowly. "Forget about other women for a minute. I want you to tell me how and why you convinced Danny to break up with me."

Watching her reaction carefully, I am rewarded. It's only there for a brief moment, but I clearly see it flash across her face. At first I think it is guilt but then I realize this is my mother we are talking about and she would never feel guilty about hurting my relationship with Danny. No, what I see is pure culpability. She panics for a split second thinking I have something on her before she schools her features back into impassivity.

"I have no clue what you're talking about, Ryan." She sounds affronted but it also sounds hollow to me.

"Don't lie to me, Mother."

"I'm not lying to you and don't you accuse me of that. It's disrespectful and I'll not tolerate that behavior from my children."

"Tell me the truth!" I yell.

I'm frustrated beyond measure and I need for her to tell me that my suspicions are correct. Because if she verifies that for me, that means I have a chance to get Danny back.

My mother stands up. "We are done with this conversation. I suggest you leave and not come back until you can show me some respect."

Turning on her heel she walks toward the door.

I try one last tactic. "If you ever even had a small measure of love for me, I'm begging you mom...please tell me the truth." My words are soft and pleading.

She pauses for just a second and I think she might turn around and tell me what I want to know, but then she continues walking toward the door and doesn't look back.

Defeated, I leave my house and I doubt I'll be returning. The painful realization that my mother doesn't care enough about me to want my happiness is starting to sink in. It's amazing how much this hurts, given the fact that I have never been very close to my parents in the first place. I guess there was a part of me that believed that some nurturing, maternal instinct would spring forth from Celia Burnham. Sadly, the fact that I was pretty much raised by our nanny should have clued me in and lowered my expectations.

✦

I'm back at the frat house and lying on my bed. Hands clasped behind my head, I need to figure out what my next move will be with Danny. My main problem is in making contact with her since she won't return my calls. I suppose I can stalk her at Sally's or at her apartment, but I'm leery of doing that until I know for sure what I'm going to say. I think this is a one-shot deal with Danny and I don't want to screw it up.

I'll have to admit I'm a little hurt she won't return my calls. I understand my mother, in all likelihood, did something atrocious to scare Danny off. But there is that one small part of me that wishes Danny cared about me enough that we could have at least remained friends.

Running through a mental list of all of the things I want to say to Danny, I'm startled when someone knocks on my door.

"Come in."

The door creaks open and my sister, Emily, peaks her head in. I'm stunned she's here. We are not very close but we do tolerate each other. As far as I can remember, I don't think she's ever been to visit me here on campus.

"Hey," I say. "What are you doing here?"

She shrugs her shoulders and doesn't say anything as she shuts the door behind herself. She's dressed in designer jeans and a lightweight sweater. Her dark hair is pulled up into a ponytail and I suddenly realize how pretty she is. She's going to break someone's heart one day.

After looking around the room, she finally sits on Mike's bed with her hands clasped in her lap.

"Can I ask you something?" she begins.

I sit up on the bed and turn to face her. I have no clue where this is going and it's a bit surreal. If I had to bet money, Mother has sent her here to do some reconnaissance.

"Sure," I tell her.

"Do you really love this girl, Danny?" She says Danny's name with a little bit of distaste but I also hear genuine curiosity. It's like love is a foreign concept to her, and maybe it is. I have no clue if Emily has ever been in love or if she is even dating someone. It makes me realize that I don't know much about her at all.

"I love Danny very much." I don't offer more because, again, I have no clue why she is here and I have to assume it's on Mother's behalf.

Emily looks down at her hands and she nervously twirls a dainty sapphire ring she is wearing. She looks back up at me. "Would you tell me why?"

This time there is nothing in her tone other than a pleading to understand something that might be beyond her concept. Maybe Emily is here because she's maturing past the elitist brat I've always assumed her to be.

I take a deep breath and give her a wistful smile. "Okay. Let's see. Do you want the list numerically or alphabetically?"

Emily lets out a very unladylike snort and immediately slaps her hand over her mouth because she can't believe she just did that. She giggles at herself which causes my eyebrows to rise. I don't think I've ever heard Emily giggle before.

Removing her hand from her mouth, she says with a grin, "In any order you want."

"Well, when I first met Danny it was her wit that got my attention. In fact, I actually heard her before I saw her...and I was captivated by her intelligence. But when I looked up, I was immediately attracted to her. I thought she was so beautiful."

"But her hair is purple and she has piercings in her face?"

There is the judgmental tone again but I have patience with her. "Why does that matter, Emily? Really, in the grand scheme of things...so what?"

Emily shrugs her shoulders. "Because it's weird I guess. No one we know looks like that."

"Well, then I'd say maybe you need to expand your horizons a bit."

I can see the wheels turning in her head as she ponders that statement. "What else?" she demands.

"She's really smart and talented. She was a music major at Julliard but had to drop out when her mother got cancer. She plays the violin and she's amazingly good. I'm trying to get her to go back."

"What else?" she whispers.

"She's kind and generous. She volunteers a few times a week at a homeless shelter. I've gone there to help her a few times and met some really interesting people."

Emily looks at me in horror over the prospect of working in a homeless shelter. Okay, so I probably will never get Emily to explore that side of her humanitarianism but it was worth a shot.

She's silent for a while, again twisting that ring of hers. She looks anxious. "Those are all really good reasons to love someone."

"Emily, they're the best reasons to love someone. Not because of some silly notions we have about class or stations in life."

Emily stands up and comes to sit beside me on my bed. She turns to look at me and her face is awash with misery.

"Danny didn't breakup with you voluntarily," she whispers. "Mother threatened you to get her to do it."

"Son of a bitch," I exclaim loudly. I had suspected this was the case, but hearing it out loud pisses me off. Emily flinches from the anger in my voice, but it doesn't scare her off for which I'm glad. She continues on.

"Mother went to see her a few weeks ago and asked me to go along. I admit...I was curious to see this girl that was causing so much trouble in our household. And I'm sorry. I looked at her and I just didn't understand what you saw in her. But I get it now."

I exhale heavily, vindicated to know the truth at last. But I need more details and my mother is not going to give them to me.

Tears are swimming in Emily's eyes and while I'm angry at her, I have to be thankful she brought this to me. I grab her in a quick hug. "Thanks, Em. That means the world that you told me the truth."

She nods her head and squeezes me back. "What else can I do to help?"

"Just tell me everything that Mother said to Danny so I can try to make this right with her and beg forgiveness of my family's stupidity."

"That's a whole lot of stupid," Emily quips and I nod in agreement.

# CHAPTER EIGHTEEN

# Danny

It's been two weeks since I've seen Ryan and I am miserable. I have to practically slap myself at least twenty times a day so I don't call him. Depression seems to be my mood of choice and its worrying Paula to death. She thinks I ought to confess everything to Ryan and beg him to take me back.

God, I so want to do that but I can't risk Ryan's mother retaliating against him. This is so fucked up.

Lying on my bed now, I stare over at the violin Ryan gave me. I laid it on my desk the day we broke up and I haven't picked it up since. I have no desire to and I'm worried that my love of music has been irrevocably broken.

The memory of the last time I played—for Ryan—is bitterly painful to me. The thoughtfulness of his gesture in getting me a violin to the look of rapture on his face when I had played for him were some of the best moments of my life and I'm pissed as hell that those are gone. Those memories are tainted now by the grief over what I've lost.

Without Ryan in my life, my desire to make music is

non-existent. It's just hard for me to imagine picking the violin back up again.

✦

I suppose I've done something to warrant the evil forces of nature targeting me with their cruel games. For the past week, Angeline and her friends have been coming to Sally's with nothing more than the sole purpose of torturing me.

As I wait on them, I hear crude snippets of conversation meant to hurt or humiliate me. I try to let it go in one ear and out the other, but it's not easy.

Just last night, as I refilled everyone's water glasses at her table, Angeline "accidentally" knocked her bowl of soup to the floor. I say "accidentally" with as much sarcasm as I can muster because in all actuality, I watched her literally slide the bowl to the edge of the table and then wait until I was within reach before she pushed it all the way over.

As I was bending over to wipe up the mess, I heard one of her cronies say, "I heard that was the position she was in when Ryan caught her and Reece Malone going at it in Ryan's bed."

I stood up and faced the table, my face red with anger that they would try to humiliate me with the fact I was nearly raped. And they were trying to make it sound like I was consensually with Reece. I looked around at their faces, and they were all smiling innocently at me. All except for Cameron. I noted she looked at me with sympathy.

I walked up and towered over Angeline. "That's a lie, Angeline and you know it. Reece Malone tried to rape me." I was seething inside.

"Oh, come on, Danny. Everyone here knows you were fucking Reece behind Ryan's back. It's the reason Ryan broke up with you. Everyone on campus is talking about it."

"No thanks to the vicious lies I'm sure you're spreading."

Angeline wasn't fazed at all. She gave a tinkling laugh and then her eyes turned hard. "Who do you think they'll believe...me or you?"

I turned my attention back to everyone at the table. "I suggest you all check your facts. Reece Malone is in jail for attempted rape."

"Well, of course he is silly," Angeline said. "We all know you claimed it was rape so Ryan wouldn't know you were screwing around on him."

Tears welled up in my eyes and Angeline's look was triumphant that she was able to break me. I heard a loud scraping sound and looked down the table. Cameron stood up abruptly. Grabbing her purse, she gave a disgusted look at Angeline and walked out of the diner.

I turned my back on the table and fled back into the kitchen. I talked another waitress into finishing my tables and left for the night.

And here I am for apparently another brutal shift. Angeline and her friends—minus Cameron—have all walked in together. They arrange themselves around two tables. There is no doubt this is a repetitive effort on her part to torment me because she never hung out in here that much prior to me meeting Ryan.

Unfortunately, I am the only one working tonight because it's a Wednesday and we are always slow in the middle of the week. I grab seven iced waters and carry them to the tables, setting them down in front of each girl.

"Do you guys know what you want," I ask.

"Hmmm..." Angeline says, perusing the menu. "I'm not sure. Of course, I'm not very hungry after the wonderful lunch I had with Ryan today. We followed it up with dessert in his room."

*I will not punch this girl, I will not punch this girl.*

Angeline puts a look of mock apology on her face.

"Oh, I'm sorry Danny. I guess that was insensitive, mentioning intimate details about Ryan to you." She snickers and the rest of her girls all titter over her jibes.

"What do you want to order, Angeline? Make it quick."

She ignores me but leans toward me conspiratorially. "Between you and me, Danny, I'm not sure you were good enough to keep Ryan interested between the sheets. He's an animal, you know. We were at it all afternoon."

Before I could respond, I hear, "That's a fucking lie, Angeline."

My heart doubles in speed as I hear his voice. Turning slowly around, I drink Ryan in as he stands there with his hands clenched and looking like he wants to murder Angeline.

He's wearing faded jeans and a long sleeve t-shirt. He has on his old, ratty Chuck-T's that I adore. He has a baseball cap on and the ends of his long hair are sticking out at adorable angles. I almost burst into tears looking at him.

I turn to glance at Angeline and she looks green in the face. In a million years, I guarantee she never thought Ryan would be in earshot of her lies.

Ryan closes the distance to the table and looks down at Angeline. "This is the one and only time I'm going to say this. And this goes for all of you sitting at this table." Ryan pauses and looks at each person. "If I so much as hear of anyone saying another bad thing about Danny, I will personally take it upon myself to have you blacklisted from every organization at this school. Furthermore, I will use the power of my family and our vast resources to ruin every one of you. There won't be a place you can hide from me. And just so everyone is perfectly clear, I did not fuck Angeline this afternoon, nor would I touch her with a ten foot pole again. Please make sure that is spread around. There is only one woman I want to touch. Because she's the one I love."

Ryan spins from the table and stalks over to me. My

mouth is hanging open and he never pauses when he pulls my head to his and crushes his mouth to mine. I know I should pull away but I can't. I love him too much. I'll worry about the consequences of this later and hope Ryan's mother doesn't find out about this.

Ryan's arms snake around my waist and he pulls me to him tight. My arms go around his neck and I hold on for dear life while he kisses me like there is no tomorrow. Then abruptly he pulls away. He looks me dead in the eyes and says, "I love you, Danny. And I can tell by that kiss you still love me. We'll talk after you get off work."

I watch astounded as Ryan goes up to the counter and sits down. He apparently is going to wait here until my shift is over. I know I should be panicking that he wants some type of confrontation tonight, but I am numb from everything that has just transpired in the last thirty seconds.

Turning my back on Angeline's crew, I walk to the other side of the counter and pull out a coffee cup. I fill it up and push it in front of Ryan. He doesn't say anything. I glance over and see that Angeline and her friends are leaving, noticeably a lot quieter than when they had arrived.

✦

Taking my apron off, I walk up to Ryan. "I'm done."

"Can I give you a ride home and then we talk?"

My gut instinct is to decline because I'm terrified his mother will find out, but I owe him the time to talk. I should have given it to him before now but I've been so afraid his mother would find out. I wouldn't put it past her to have hired a damn private investigator to keep tabs on us.

"Sure."

The ride to my place is tense and silent. As we walk into my apartment, I quietly say over my shoulder, "Thank you for getting Angeline to back off of me. It was getting harder to keep my cool."

"It's no problem. Cameron came to me last night and told me what Angeline was doing. It was best that I confronted her and try to put a stop to it."

We sit in the living room, on opposite ends of the couch. Ryan is leaning back, looking extremely comfortable. I'm wound tight and ready to bolt.

"I miss you," he says to me.

I can feel the burn of tears and I swallow hard to tamp them down. "Ryan...please don't..."

"And you miss me, too."

He says it so matter-of-factly, like there's no room for argument. He knows me well but I decide to act incensed. "You have quite an ego to presume to think I miss you, too."

He laughs at me. Full out, gut busting laughter. I cross my arms and just wait for him to finish. After he finally winds it down, he looks at me with amusement. "We're ending this farce tonight, Danny. I'm not leaving until we are back together and you admit you love me. In fact, I promise, before this evening ends I'll make love to you."

I start sputtering. I'm half incensed and half turned on. "You are certifiable, Ryan Burnham. If you think you can just waltz in here and—"

Ryan cuts me off by launching across the couch and coming on top of me. He grips my head in his hands and kisses me. His tongue immediately ignites a fire in me and I struggle for just an instant and then I'm kissing him back. Oh God, how I missed this. His touch, his voice, his smell.

Ryan pulls back only slightly with his lips still lightly resting against mine. "I knew that would be the only way to get you to shut up."

I'm dazed from the flood of emotions coursing through me.

"Danny, I know what my mother did," Ryan says.

I sit up straight and push him backward. "You do?"

"Yeah. Emily came to me and told me."

I look over to the grouping of pictures on my end table, and stare blankly at them. I'm not sure what this means. Wait, I do know what this means. It doesn't change anything. Ryan's mom has a standing edict. I cannot be with him or she will see he gets ruined.

"That doesn't mean anything, Ryan. We can't be together."

Ryan takes a deep breath and exhales it, like he's getting ready to talk to a four year old. "Danny...I'm a little disappointed in you that you would let anything my mother would say keep us apart."

That catches me off guard. It's somewhat of an attack on me and I immediately bristle.

"I had no choice," I hiss. "She promised she could get the criminal charges against you dropped but would only do so if I stayed away. She was willing to let you take the chance of getting convicted and possibly going to jail, just to spite you if you stayed with me."

Ryan's shaking his head. "She played you, Danny. She had nothing to do with getting the charges dropped. I did that all myself."

I'm stunned. "You did?"

"Yup."

"But...but your mom said she'd ruin you if I stayed with you. Said that she would ensure you never made it to the NHL."

Ryan is now wearing a smirk on his face. "Played again."

It's like he's enjoying my stupidity.

"You don't have to be so smug over what an idiot I am," I snap.

Ryan's smirk is replaced by soberness. He grabs my hand and brings my fingers to his lips. I try to pull away but he holds firm. "Danny, I'm not laughing at you for falling for my mother's lies. I'm smirking because now that this is all out in the open, we can be together again. I'm deliriously happy."

I shake my head. "But won't your mother cut you off? Or ruin your hockey career?"

"Cut me off from what? Family ties that are brittle and based on duty and obligation rather than love. Tell me exactly what I'd be missing? And trust me, my mother doesn't have any power over my hockey career. She's blowing smoke."

I can't think of anything to say. He continues on, "More importantly, look at what we stand to lose if we bend to my mother's whim."

Hope is starting to build inside of me and I look at him. His beautiful eyes suck me in. He pulls me to him, wrapping his arms around my waist. "You are more important to me than anything else in this world. As long as I have you, I don't need anything else. It's you Danny. It will only ever be you."

Oh, Ryan. My Ryan. My hands are shaking as I bring them up to his face. I stroke his jaw and his cheek. He closes his eyes at my touch and I start feeling elation rise up in me like helium filling a balloon. My head is swimming with the possibilities of a future with my one and only.

I push up on his chest and straddle his lap. I lay my forehead against his. "Is this for real?" I whisper.

"It is," he confirms as he grips my hips, his fingers digging in deliciously.

"Oh, Ryan. I am so, so sorry I put us through this. I should have come to you first." I start crying, burdened with the weight of the hurt and pain I have unnecessarily caused this man. My love. "I never meant those horrid things I said to you."

"Sssshhh," he croons as he wipes my tears. "No more apologies. Today is the first day of the rest of our lives together."

I nod, the movement of my head pushing my lips into his. I take advantage and whisper a kiss on his mouth. He opens his mouth slightly and I run my tongue on the edge of his lips.

Kissing my way across his cheek to his ear, I tell him how much I love him.

Nibbling on his neck, I promise never to leave him again.

As his hands work their magic on me, his kisses bind me to him forever.

As our breathing becomes rough and our whispers hoarse, I beg him to make love to me.

And before the night is through, he does.

# EPILOGUE

# Ryan
*15 Months Later*

I wake up and glance at the alarm clock.

5:52 a.m.

It's going to go off in eight minutes and I groan inwardly. Freakin' early mornings. Reaching over, I flip the switch to turn it off. Then I roll over to the soft bundle sleeping next to me. *My Danny.*

She's laying on her right side with her back to me. Her left arm is tucked to her chest, her fist resting under her chin. She's snoring softly—a fact I learned she did quite frequently after we moved in together, but I think it's adorable. I slide over and press the front of my body to her back then wrap my arm around her to pull her even closer. She lets out a little sigh then resumes snoring. I smile to myself and bury my nose in her neck. She smells like sunshine to me. Always sunshine.

I place a kiss on her shoulder —so gentle —I'll be the only one to ever know it was there.

Reluctantly, I slide out of bed. There's nothing more I would rather do than roll Danny under me and bury myself in her but she was up late last night studying and she needs the sleep.

As I pad into the bathroom, I smile thinking about her. She re-enrolled in Julliard and will graduate this coming spring. She has been studying hard and playing her violin even harder. Her delicate finger tips are now hard with callouses, but they still make me shiver when she drags them across my skin. I am so proud of her and of course, we are both incredibly lucky that I signed to play hockey with the New York Rangers. I honestly don't know what I would have done if I couldn't join a New York team so that I could be near Danny. For me, it was out of the question that Danny would go anywhere but Julliard. I would accept nothing less.

Turning on the shower, I strip out of my boxers. I go ahead and shave while the shower is heating up, grinning at the lucky fool staring back at me in the mirror. Danny and I had many discussions, and some heated fights, about her music career. She insisted she could go to school anywhere and thus could be with me wherever I ended up playing hockey. That didn't set well with me. Danny is so talented...she deserves to be at Julliard. By some miracle, the New York Rangers wanted me and Julliard gladly accepted Danny back.

So here we are, living in Manhattan, in a small two-bedroom apartment that conveniently sits almost smack dab in the middle of Julliard and Madison Square Gardens. And my life is almost perfect.

Almost.

✦

I finished a short run this morning just to get my muscles loose. I have a team meeting in a few hours to prepare for tonight's game. The fantastic hockey I've been playing has earned me a spot on the Rangers' second line and it's a dream come true for me. Almost as good as having Danny in my life.

Bundled up in a fuzzy yellow robe, Danny softly walks into the living room while I'm watching ESPN Sports Center. I set my coffee down and open my arms. She has that sleepy look in her eyes and she crawls onto my lap to snuggle in.

"Did you get some good sleep?" I ask.

"Mmmm. Hmmmm," she purrs as she nods her head up and down against my chest. I reach my hand up and smooth some of the tangles in her hair.

"I'm glad. You've been burning the midnight oil quite a bit, baby."

As if to just prove my point, she stretches her arms out and gives a loud yawn. Then she tucks back in to my body. I turn my attention back to Sports Center, trying to get up to speed on all the highlights. It seems to be the only time I can get to find out what is going on in the sports world.

Danny tilts her head up and places a soft kiss on the edge of my jaw. "Did you hear back from your parents yet?"

I clench my teeth and just shake my head at her. I invited my parents to the game tonight as my father is giving a speech in New York tomorrow. I didn't really expect them to accept the invite, because hey, they've declined all of the other invitations Danny and I have extended to them. My mother is still staunchly against my relationship with Danny and my father does whatever my mother tells him to do. I would never have invited them at all, but Danny's big heart keeps pushing me to do it. She has faith that, with time, my mother will come around. I wish I could be more like Danny. Her unwavering belief in the human spirit is boundless.

She doesn't say anything more nor does she try to push the subject. I hold her gently while watching TV and before long, I've forgotten all about my parents.

Just as the Sports Center episode is finishing, there is a knock at our door. I look down at my watch.

*Right on time.*

"Do you mind getting the door, honey?" I ask her as I stand up from the couch, dislodging her from my lap. "I'll start making some breakfast."

I smile as Danny grumbles at me but she gets up and walks to the door. I stand just outside the kitchen, my body leaning up against the wall and I watch her. She unlocks the deadbolt and swings the door open. I watch as stunned disbelief slides over her face. Standing on the other side of the threshold is her best friend, Paula. I flew her in from Boston to spend the weekend as a surprise for Danny.

Danny finally comes to her senses and lets out a piercing shriek. Paula answers her with an equally loud squawk of her own. I wince. These two women both put nails on a chalkboard to shame.

Now they are hugging each other and rocking back and forth with joy. It's been almost six months since we moved here and I know Danny misses Paula a lot.

Before I realize it, Danny is releasing Paula and hurtling across the room to me. She jumps in my arms, locking those gorgeous legs around my waist and hugs me tight. Lust shoots through me having her pressed up against my groin and I try to think of something gross to prevent me from getting a hard-on while Paula stands there and watches us. *Slugs, vomit, snot.* Yup. That works.

"You are such a sneak, Ryan Burnham," Danny accuses me. "How did you pull this off without me knowing it?"

I chuckle and kiss her lightly, squeezing her ass because...well, I can and she's all mine. "I hate to tell you, babe, you're not that observant. It was easy enough arranging this."

I let Danny slide to the floor and then Paula gives me a big hug. She doesn't scare me as much as she used to. We've sort of bonded over our mutual love of and need to protect Danny. I turn and leave them to their reunion and head to the kitchen to make us all breakfast.

# Danny

I love Madison Square Gardens. There's an actual vibrating buzz of excitement in the air as over 17,000 fans wait for the game to start. Paula is sitting next to me, happily chewing on a hot dog. I still can't believe Ryan flew her here for the weekend. Just when I didn't think it was possible to love him anymore, he goes and does this crap. He's impossible and he's mine.

Normally, when I come to Ryan's home games, I sit further up in the stands, but I guess Ryan wanted to make it special with Paula being here. Tonight, our seats are on the ice, just to the side of the Rangers' bench. Now I can get a close up view of my honey at work.

We're still waiting on Ryan's sister, Emily. She usually goes with me to every home game. She's in her first year at Columbia and totally loves New York. I don't see her ever leaving it. And it's amazing how much our relationship has grown. Those girlfriend/sister lunch dates I had once fantasized about have come true. I mean, Emily still has her issues, and she's actually trying to break away a bit from her mother's domineering ways. Overall, she's actually a very sweet girl but sometimes I can see a little of Celia Burnham peeking through. The fact that she and Ryan have grown closer over the past few months makes my heart sing.

I look at Paula. God, I miss her so much.

"So how have you been doing?" I ask her.

"Just peachy. Work at the record store is...well, boring as shit but what's a girl to do. How about you?"

I sigh. My life is freakin' fantastic and I keep waiting to wake up from this dream. "There are no words, Paula. I'm studying music again and I'm with the man of my dreams. I don't think the English language has enough adjectives to describe my feelings."

"You are such a dork," she replies.

"Harpy."

"Rhinoceros."

"Bilbo Baggins."

I think I have her with this one but she remains stone-faced. Then she gets me when she leans over to me and starts singing...really, really loud.

*"Why do you build me up*
*Buttercup baby just to*
*let me down*
*And mess me around*
*And then worst of all*
*You never call baby*
*When you say you will*
*But I love you still*
*I need you*
*More than anyone darlin'*
*You know that I have from the start."*

I bust out laughing and notice a smattering of applause from the people around us. Paula just smirks at me and I lean over and give her a quick hug. Yes, I have missed her terribly.

"Oh, God. Please don't tell me I have to sing just to sit with you two?"

I look up and see Emily standing there. She's stunning with her glossy dark hair and those same bourbon eyes that Ryan has. She's wearing her brother's jersey —#73 — just like me.

I stand up and give Emily a quick hug and she sits down next to me. She knows Paula but not enough to give her a hug so they both just mutter, "Hey" to each other. And now I'm ready to get on with the show. I want to see my man.

✦

I don't know if it will ever change but every time I see

155

Ryan step out from the tunnel and skate onto the ice, my body quivers. It must be part nerves but if I'm honest with myself, it mostly has to do with the fact that he's just so damned hot in his uniform. And I could not be prouder of him. He made it to the NHL and his dreams have all come to fruition. The man is simply amazing and he deserves every bit of it.

Ryan skates by, giving me a little wink and my smile stretches from ear to ear. I'm vaguely aware of Emily and Paula talking but my focus is on Ryan. I get so nervous for him on game days. Today, before he headed over to the arena, he seemed a little off. I'm assuming he was just anxious about the game, which is understandable. They are playing the Pittsburgh Penguins and they are #1 in the Atlantic Division.

I'm surprised when the lights in the arena dim just slightly and the announcer says in that deep baritone voice, "Will Danny Cross please turn your attention to the Jumbotron at center ice."

Suddenly, a spotlight is on me and I feel a million prickles run across my skin. My face immediately heats up with embarrassment as if I just got busted sneaking in after curfew. I drag my gaze up to the giant scoreboard and the screen shows the camera is focused on me, Paula and Emily. I take note of the stunned expression on my face and Paula is waving happily at the camera. Emily just has her mouth turned up in a smirk.

What. The. Hell? Did they do this as a prank?

Before I can turn to them to ask, the video of us blacks out and the words "You Are My One and Only" flash onto the screen. My breath catches in my lungs and my head is literally buzzing. That's what Ryan and I call each other. I have no clue what is going on but I sense it's something big.

And then Ryan is on the video. He's in his uniform and the video only shows him from the waist up. I glance out to the ice but with the lights dimmed, I cannot see him.

And then Ryan starts talking on the monitor.

"Danny...you are my one and only...just as I am yours. My life with you is almost perfect...but not quite. The only way to make that happen is if you will agree to be my wife." He takes a pause, then a deep breath, and then he says with the most devilish smile on his face, "And I figure if I asked you in front of all of these people, you would never embarrass me by saying no. So will you?"

The screen blanks out for a second and then the video comes back up of me sitting there in my seat, looking bewildered. Paula and Emily are looking at me expectantly. The arena is eerily quiet.

Then I hear from just behind me. "So, will you?"

I swing around and Ryan is standing there in the aisle —just a foot behind my seat —in all his full hockey regalia. His smile is gone and he is looking like he might be sick any moment if I don't say something. He reaches out and I see he has a black velvet box in his hand. He opens it up and inside is the most exquisite diamond ring I have ever seen. The sparkles flying off of it are in danger of causing me to have a seizure. I stand up and step out into the aisle, staring into those copper eyes. I see promise, hope and love shining back at me. I see my future and my salvation.

Everything seems to be in slow motion and I hear a few people scream out, "Say yes!"

I walk up to the step where Ryan stands and then walk past him to the step above. He turns his body, following my movement and I'm sure he thinks I may be bolting. But I'm not. I just want to put myself within better reaching distance to his enormous height.

And then I launch myself at him, wrapping my arms around his neck and burying my face just below his jaw. "Yes, Ryan. I will marry you."

His arms tighten around me and I pull my head back. There is so much emotion vibrating between us, I half expect him to give me a scorching X-rated kiss. But I'm sure he remembers the cameras are on us and he instead feathers the softest kiss on my lips, followed by one on my forehead.

The arena erupts into cheers and Ryan releases his hold on me. He takes the ring and puts it on my finger.

"I love you so much," he says softly, so only I can hear.

I stare at the ring for only a second but then look back into his beautiful eyes. "I love you, too. Now get back out on that ice and kick some Penguin ass."

He throws a dazzling smile at me, slaps me on the butt and hustles off. I watch him until he disappears from sight and I wish that my parents could have been here to see this.

I glance around me and everyone is cheering and smiling at me. Paula and Emily walk up and wrap me in fierce hugs, grabbing my hand to look at the ring. Complete strangers reach out to clap me on the back. I have all of this emotion and vibrancy swirling around me. My heartbeat is working overtime and I'm actually a little dizzy from the onslaught of sensation.

I swing my gaze back to the ice and I see Ryan is down there skating again.

Just looking at him, I immediately feel myself calm. Everything comes back into focus. Unbelievable warmth and peace suffuses through me.

All because of my Ryan...my one and only.

# ABOUT THE AUTHOR

Sawyer Bennett is the pen name for a native North Carolinian and practicing lawyer. When not trying to save the world from injustice, she spends her time trying to get the stories she accumulates in her head down on paper. She lives in North Carolina with her husband, Shawn, and their two big dogs, Piper and Atticus.

Help end Veteran homelessness:
http://va.gov/homeless/help_a_homeless_veteran_general.asp?gclid=COK6veTPvbUCFQPnnAodTm0Aow

CPSIA information can be obtained
at www.ICGtesting.com
Printed in the USA
LVOW08s1539240317
528385LV00003B/478/P